"I REMEMBER NOTHING,"

Lucinda said. "Why am I here?"

"Can't you recall?" asked the countess.

"I can't remember at all." She put one hand to her head, her eyes opening wide in horror. "I don't even know who I am!"

Lucinda looked at the countess. She reached out and touched her arm. "Who am I and what am I doing here? Please, I beg of you, tell me!"

The countess swallowed the lump in her throat. Then she asked in a very deliberate voice, "Do you not remember travelling from London?"

The girl shook her head. "Please, tell me who I am. I remember nothing."

The countess drew herself up straight. "You are my son's wife—the new Countess of Glenbrooke."

RECKLESS
MASQUERADE

A NOVEL BY

Rachelle Edwards

A FAWCETT CREST BOOK

Fawcett Publications, Inc., Greenwich, Connecticut

RECKLESS MASQUERADE

THIS BOOK CONTAINS THE COMPLETE TEXT OF THE ORIGINAL HARDCOVER EDITION.

A Fawcett Crest Book reprinted by arrangement with Robert Hale & Company

ISBN: 0-449-23302-2

Printed in the United States of America

10 9 8 7 6 5 4 3 2 1

Chapter One

It was already late afternoon and the inn was crowded with travellers who were eager to assuage their hunger and slake a thirst caused by hours of dusty travelling along bumpy roads. It was the dinner hour but most travellers on their way north or south were glad enough of an excuse to stop for a while, to rest after a jolting even the best sprung carriage could not mitigate.

One of those glad of the respite was Lucinda Kendricks. Her destination was Wakefield in the north of England, and she would not reach it until the following day. She was sitting at a large table, sandwiched between a corpulent farmer who ate, scorning the spoon put before him for his use, as fast as the food was put before him, and a schoolboy, although slim, who did likewise. It was almost, but not quite, as uncomfortable as the stage and Lucinda wondered if she would survive the remainder of the journey.

It was her first journey by stage—her first journey anywhere that she could remember. Having been placed in a charity institution at the tender age of four years, Lucinda wished she could have stayed there indefinitely. But Mrs Cressington's daughter needed someone to help with her children, and Mrs Cressington was a patroness of the orphanage. Besides, Lucinda had remained at the orphanage far beyond the usual age limit, only because she was so good with the younger children. She was fortunate not to have been put into service long ago. And this position, she continually reminded herself, was an exceedingly good one. She might even be treated almost as one of the family if she was lucky.

The schoolboy paused in his eating to offer Lucinda a dish of boiled pork. Lucinda despite the shabby hand-me-down gown she wore was a remarkably pretty girl. Her honey-coloured hair curled naturally, her eyes were as green as emeralds, and her skin was as flawless as the petals of the roses which were now beginning to bloom all over the King's fair country. And the schoolboy was of an age to appreciate such attributes. But Lucinda shook her head. It was all she could do to pick forlornly at a breast of chicken. Travelling as she did, on the roof of the stage, made her constantly nauseous, and although it was late into the spring being an outside passenger was a cold business. Her fingers were still numb after clinging on for hours and her cheeks still stung from the dusty bite of the wind.

And Lucinda was apprehensive about her future. She hadn't wanted to leave the orphanage. The thought of going out into the world frightened her beyond belief, and if the existence at the orphan asylum had been sparse, Lucinda knew of no other life; and no one had ever been unkind to her there.

She had hoped to remain there for the rest of her life, to continue helping with the younger children, which was something she loved to do. But Mrs Cressington had been impressed by her and she'd had no option but to accept the position offered to her. For the princely sum of ten guineas a year Lucinda was engaged to look after Mrs Purvey's three young children until they became of an age to attend a respectable academy. Beyond that Lucinda could not foresee. She supposed she would have to move on to another establishment.

A comfortable-looking matron at the far side of the table was washing down her repast with a tankard of ale. Lucinda felt her eyes pricking with sleep and yet she was able to notice with great clarity the grease marks and the ale stains on the table cloth. Travel to one unused to it was a tiring business, but Lucinda dared not doze for fear she should fall off the coach.

The schoolboy tucked heartily into a dish of blancmange. Lucinda watched his zeal with envy.

Even though the food set out for the travellers was far more plentiful than anything she had ever enjoyed at St Mary's Asylum for Needy Children, she could not partake of it as she wished she might.

The farmer, having finished his meal, sat back on the bench and began to pick his teeth. Now that his hunger was satisfied he had time to notice the pretty young girl at his side. Much to Lucinda's discomfort he began to ogle her in a way she did not like. Before leaving the orphanage she had been given a lecture on the evils that could befall her whilst she was abroad alone and this had in no way decreased her apprehension, but she had hardly expected being plagued during the journey from London to Wakefield.

She endured his leering for some minutes but when, aided by the closeness at which they were forced to sit, he began to press his thigh against hers with more urgency than proximity decreed, Lucinda struggled to her feet. She snatched up her bonnet and gloves and walked out of the dinner room and into the corridor. There was still a considerable way to go before they reached Newark that night and Lucinda looked forward to the journey with no enthusiasm.

She walked slowly along the passage towards the yard where all the carriages were waiting. It seemed, as she stretched her spine, every bone in her body ached and possibly by now she was quite badly bruised.

From the coffee room came the sounds of revelry. Lucinda in her state of weariness allowed herself to be buffeted against the wall by a half-drunken buck who came racing out of the coffee room pursued by one of his cronies.

She managed to steady herself on the handle of a half-open door to a private parlour. When she straightened up again and regained her breath she found that her bonnet had been flattened against the wall. She gave a little gasp of dismay; the bonnet was an old one which had once belonged to Mrs Cressington's personal maid, but it was the only one she possessed and she wished to arrive at her destination in some degree of order.

Angrily, and almost tearfully, she straightened out the brim and placed it on top of her curls. As she tied the ribbons into place she glanced, a little warily, into the parlour for fear she had disturbed the occupant. But she need not have worried. Whoever occupied the room had not stirred, as was evident by the pair of highly polished Hessians which remained outstretched by the fire, and an untouched meal which lay on the table.

The rest of the occupant Lucinda could not see but she allowed herself a small sigh of relief and drew away. As she did so the man moved out of his chair by the fire. She froze and gazed at him in fascination, for she had rarely seen a man of such elegance and style. On occasions she had chanced to see a gentleman of the *beau monde* racing down a London street in his curricle or high-perch phaeton. Those occasions were rare but now she was able to recognise Quality when she saw it. His coat was of the finest cut, his pale buff pantaloons wrinkle free, and his neckcloth intricately folded. His carriage had an almost indefinable quality about it but it declared him, to Lucinda, an aristocrat.

As he turned and began to pace restlessly up and down the room, she saw that he was also an extremely handsome fellow, with dark curls carefully coaxed into a seemingly careless style. His eyes were of the darkest brown and his nose straight, not a mite too long or too short.

He seemed preoccupied as he paced the floor, quite unaware that someone was watching him, although he had only to glance up in order to see her. He was undoubtedly troubled as was indicated by his deep frown, and Lucinda fleetingly wondered what problems could possibly afflict a man so obviously well-endowed.

She had no chance to deliberate on any speculations, for just at that moment her fellow travellers came hurrying out of the dinner room at the back of the inn. Lucinda drew away from the doorway, feeling slightly ashamed at having spied upon the gentleman unobserved. She began to follow her fellow travellers out into the yard and as she came out into the chilly sunlight she had no time to blink at its unexpected assault on her eyes, for she was grasped by a fat and sweaty hand about her waist.

"Yer needs a bit o' flesh on yer bones," said the

fat farmer in her ear, "but yer'll do all right for me."

Lucinda struggled to free herself from his obnoxious grasp but was unable to do so. Indeed, her struggling enabled him to pull her even closer against his stained coat which smelled quite offensively of an accumulation of sweat and dirt and ale stains.

"Pray let me go, sir," she gasped.

"Now then, don't struggle, m'dear," he said, chuckling to himself. "I be seeing you sittin' a top the coach all these miles. Wouldn't it be more comfy for yer to sit inside along with me?"

His eyes narrowed fractionally as he waited for her reply. A more worldly creature would have considered being pinched and cuddled for a few miles small enough price to pay for the comparative luxury of a seat inside the coach. But at such a suggestion Lucinda was even more nauseated. She could even feel his foul breath on her cheek.

"Certainly not!" she retorted, struggling anew.

"Don't do to be too top-lofty, miss," said the farmer, not relinquishing his hold on her. "I bet you got a real pretty smile when you've a mind to flash the ivories, m'beauty."

Lucinda managed to free herself at last and pulled thankfully away, only to be caught by the arm in his vice-like grip. His smile was now thin-lipped and cruel and she was beginning to be thoroughly frightened.

"Don't do to be facy with Jem Miller," he said through his teeth.

Lucinda twisted her arm in an effort to free it as the man drew her inexorably closer. Just at that moment an expertly wielded riding whip flicked through the air to crack down on Jem Miller's hand. Immediately, as she screamed in surprise, her arm was freed.

For a moment or two she did not know what had happened and she looked about her in alarm. The unfortunate farmer had sprung away from her with a degree of agility even he was not aware he possessed, and was now nursing his wrist and snarling in pain, having forgotten everything but his momentary agony.

Lucinda turned round to see that the young man who had been in the private parlour was now advancing towards them. He was now wearing a caped driving coat over his fashionable attire, and at a rakish angle a curly-brimmed beaver atop his shining locks.

He ignored Lucinda completely, his eyes being on the farmer who backed away a few more steps. There was anger in the young man's demeanour but his dark eyes were icy cold.

"I believe the young lady has indicated her distaste for your company," he said in a voice which, although low and impossible to be heard by others about the yard, carried enough conviction to drain the colour from the farmer's usually ruddy countenance.

The farmer opened his mouth to speak but in view of the attack from a man of such evident consequence no words issued forth. He could cope with naive young women travelling the country alone, but he knew well that some of these young bucks could kill a man with little effort and less justification just for the fun of it.

He turned to hurry into the waiting stage but jumped violently as the whip touched him lightly again. He stopped in his tracks, his eyes wide with fear as the gentleman sauntered up to him. Lucinda pressed one gloved hand to her lips to stifle a chuckle. How splendid it was to see a bully made to cower.

"I trust," said the gentleman, displaying an air of languor, "that the lady will have no cause for complaint from now onwards."

The farmer, still wide-eyed, shook his head. "No sir, that she won't, m'lord ... yer grace."

The young man smiled, but his eyes remained cold. "Oh, 'my lord' will suffice. I have no wish to be elevated beyond my station."

Lucinda's eyes were now wide with admiration at how a few simple words could do so much more than mere fisticuffs.

The young man's smile faded as he fondled the whip between his fingers. "If the lady is molested any further be assured I shall hear of it and you will answer to me for it, my man. And I can assure you I make no idle boasts. Is that understood?"

The farmer nodded, as if mesmerised by the young man's steely stare. Lucinda clasped her gloved hands together in front of her. She was enjoying herself hugely.

"Well, be off with you then!" ordered her rescuer and as the farmer scrambled into the stage, thankful to be let off so lightly, he turned to walk away.

"That was kind of you, sir," murmured Lucinda, starting forward when it seemed he was about to pass her without so much as a glance.

He paused and eyed her with a bored glance which, because it lingered, caused her cheeks to flush crimson, and then bowing slightly he said, "I was glad to have been of service to you, ma'am."

With that he strode away, leaping into a bright yellow curricle standing a few yards from the stage. A group of scruffy young boys who always infested the courtyards of coaching inns, stood back to let him through. A tiger in blue and gold livery handed his master the ribbons before jumping up behind him. The team of horses pawed impatiently at the ground and were off at a spanking pace the moment they were given their head.

Still somewhat bemused after that encounter, Lucinda watched the curricle through the archway and out of sight, which took a very few seconds because of its speed. The coachman in his red box coat had been helping a new passenger, a man with much luggage, on to the coach and when she glanced upwards she drew a sigh, knowing she would have even less room up there this time.

The coachman helped her climb up. She settled herself as comfortably as she could, wishing she could have thanked her unknown rescuer more profoundly. She had heard so many evil tales of the vices of such men of fashion, it was a surprise to find one willing to help a lady in distress without taking advantage of her himself. Still, if she were honest with herself he had hardly noticed her, and he had gained a vindictive pleasure from chastising the farmer. At the memory of how the farmer had been summarily dealt with, she felt an unfamiliar flush of pleasure. In other circumstances she might have felt sorry for the wretched man.

She drew a little sigh of resignation, knowing she was never likely to see the young man again. She glanced around her, putting the encounter firmly from her mind. The Leicestershire countryside was freshly green and luxuriant, so different to the grey walls and smoky chimney tops she was used to. Incredibly she had never seen the countryside before; her only knowledge of it was gained from as many books as she could manage to read.

If she hadn't been forced to spend so many hours in this uncomfortable position, if the wind hadn't made her cheeks smart and her eyes water, and if the dust from the road had not flown up and almost choked her, she might have derived some enjoyment from the unparalleled views of the countryside which she had, up until then, only been able to imagine.

Very close to her the inn sign swung gently in the breeze, creaking a little on its hinges. As she glanced at it she tightened her pelisse around her, to ward off the chill which would come as night gradually enveloped them. Her gaze was once more drawn to the inn sign. The inn was called "The King's Executioner" and the sign bore a painting of a man in Tudor costume. He was a cold-eyed individual who made Lucinda want to shiver at the sight of him, but as she gazed at the sign in fascination, she fancied the face looked familiar.

One of the ostlers standing by the coach noticed her interest. He smiled cheekily and said, "Rum cove, ain't he?"

Lucinda smiled at him. "He certainly is. Who is he? I fancy I've seen him somewhere before."

" 'Appen you 'ave, miss. You were just talkin' to one of the Farringdons. This bloke's the first Earl of Glenbrooke, Jeremiah Farringdon."

"I understand now," said Lucinda, realising at last from whom the young man had inherited his cold demeanour and the menacing air that had immediately cowed the farmer.

"Why, then, is he called the king's executioner?"

The ostler grinned again. "That's as how he was a friend of Good King Harry."

Lucinda frowned. "King Henry the Eighth?"

"That'll be the one. It's said that every time the king wanted someone under the ground all he had to do was tell Jeremiah Farringdon and the deed was as good as done." He winked conspiratorially. "Quietly like." He passed his forefinger across his throat in a graphic gesture which made Lucinda shudder.

"How horrible."

The ostler grinned again and then a moment later when a postchaise swept into the courtyard he rushed off to attend to it.

So, she thought with pride, it was no other than the Earl of Glenbrooke who had come to her aid so gallantly. A little thrill of pleasure ran down her spine at the memory of how he had bowed to her as if she were a lady worthy of his attention, be it only momentarily. She might have known he was a man of such consequence; his whole bearing proclaimed it loudly.

Lucinda wondered if he were as wicked as it was said his ancestor had been. She doubted it. If he were, he would have simply enjoyed watching the farmer have his sport with her. She had seen young bucks in the streets of London enjoying such spectacles before, as well as participating in them.

The coachman climbed on to the box, causing Lucinda to think then of nothing more than the next part of the journey. With a flick of his whip and a jerk of the reins the stagecoach set off on yet another leg of its journey north, with Lucinda and the other outside passengers clinging on for dear life.

Dareth Farringdon, seventh Earl of Glenbrooke, urged his team on at a faster pace. He didn't quite know why he had halted at "The King's Executioner" when he was so near his home. Certainly it had not been hunger, for he had been hard-pressed to touch a morsel of the tempting array the landlord had put before him. He had to admit to himself, however, as had been the case for a month past, he had no great wish to see his mother and admit defeat to her face. She would be aware of his failure already, but he would still have to endure her reproaches and her distress which would almost match his own.

Guilt too increased his reluctance to return home at this moment. For almost a year, since his father's death, he had idled the months away at his usual pursuits. He had enjoyed gambling at White's and Boodles', the races at Newmarket, the parading of his superb horses in Hyde Park, prize fights in various parts of the country, he had attended Drury Lane and Covent Garden, and to keep up appearances endured the usually insipid company at Almack's.

He had done no more than dance with the ladies there and sometimes cast a flirtatious eye or utter a complimentary word to those worthy of it. That was the crux of the whole matter. He had dissipated the past year in pleasurable pursuits when he should have been more serious in his intent. He needed a bride by the time he reached the age of thirty; the acquiring of one should have been his only quest this year.

The earl could not prevent a smile touching his lips now. Instead, he had spent much of his time with a woman more to his taste. Emily Cartwright was a full-blooded, passionate woman; a woman sought after by the young bucks of the town. A woman so popular she could choose her patrons carefully. A woman who gave him no taste for the heiresses who sought a suitable husband at Almack's.

He drew a small sigh which was lost on the wind. No amount of dallying at roadside inns would alter the fact that having almost reached the age of thirty he had returned to Glenbrooke Abbey without a bride. His chosen wife, Caroline Kingsley, had at the last moment refused his offer, thus dashing his hopes and a great deal of his pride.

The earl drew in the ribbons a little, thus slowing the pace of his team. The horses were tired despite their rest at the inn, so it would not do to drive them too hard now his estate was almost in view. The four matched greys had cost him a thousand pounds apiece at Tattersall's and he could not afford to endanger them.

His thoughts wandered aimlessly. He could not understand why he had troubled to interfere between the vulgar farmer and that green girl back at the inn. After all, such scenes were quite commonplace. It was not the first time he had seen a young woman accosted at a roadside inn. Of course, it was rare to find one so unwilling as this girl appeared to be.

Fleetingly he wondered what circumstances had compelled one so unworldly to travel alone. On the rare occasions it was necessary, it was usual to find a respectable matron to escort a maid, unless the girl was of very low origins and, despite her appallingly shabby attire, Glenbrooke could not believe that to be the case.

He smiled to himself again. Perhaps he was becoming sentimental, although he doubted it. Certainly it was a trait he had never before exhibited.

Unconsciously he urged his team faster. The road had long since been passing through Glenbrooke land. Whatever was to become of the future, now it felt good to be going back to Glenbrooke Abbey. London and all its attractions drew him endlessly but there were times when the demands of Society become too much for even so hardened a Corinthian as the earl.

The curricle, a recent purchase, swerved round a bend in the road but unfortunately at that very same moment a postchaise came in the opposite direction on its way south. The earl instinctively swerved into the side of the road to avoid a collision. The postchaise continued on its way but one of the curricle's wheels caught on the edge of a ditch and came to a halt, half in and half out of it.

The earl swore loudly as his curricle jolted to a standstill. Being a member of the exclusive Four-in-hand Club he was acknowledged to be one of the best whips in the country, so this lapse was doubly humiliating for him. Up until that moment the earl was sure he could have handled any vehicle in any situation, especially on roads as familiar as this one.

As soon as the curricle had jerked lopsidedly to a halt, the tiger jumped down and said encouragingly a moment later, "The wheel's not cracked, m'lord."

The earl stared down at his servant. "Damn the wheel, Bracknell! See to the cattle."

Both men were united in their concern for the greys but a moment later they were satisfied no harm had come to them.

The earl removed his curly-brimmed beaver and ruffled his curls absently. "Let's get it out, Bracknell. I've delayed long enough, and now I'm in a fever to be home."

He replaced his hat and in a very few moments he and his servant had led the team across the road and put the carriage on a level once again. It could plainly be seen that the curricle, once it had been restored to an upright position on the road, had suffered only minimal damage in the form of several scratches to its coachwork.

As the earl ran his hand across the damaged surface, Bracknell said, "We'll have that fixed quicker than hell would scorch a feather, m'lord."

Suddenly the earl's head came up at the sound of hooves pounding down the road beyond the bend around which he had just come.

"Good lord!" he said a moment later. "The stage!"

Before he had any chance to jump up and move the curricle out of the way, the stagecoach came thundering round the corner. The earl jumped back and closed his eyes in anticipation of a horrendous accident, but a moment later, when he opened them again, they widened in surprise. The driver of the stage was obviously an expert whip, for he had brought the stage to a halt with not an inch to spare.

"What's amiss there?" asked the coach driver as he jumped down from the box.

The earl allowed himself a deep breath of relief before replying, "My wheel became caught in a ditch. I had only just brought the curricle back to the road when you came round the corner." He strode up to the driver and began to pump his hand. "Allow me to congratulate you. That was an excellent piece of driving as I've ever seen."

The driver at such extravagant praise from one so eminent as the famed Earl of Glenbrooke, was almost overwhelmed and, for once, speechless. The earl was unbelievably relieved that an almost unavoidable accident had been missed, but he was now anxious to be away from the scene.

"I shall move my carriage," he told the driver as he walked away, "and you can be on your way again. You must be behind schedule now anyway."

"Hey, just a minute there!"

The earl turned and raised an eyebrow at so imperious a command coming from the inside of the coach.

"Watch yer impudence!" roared the coach driver to the schoolboy who was poking his head out of the coach window.

"But someone's fallen off the back!" the boy protested.

The driver, followed very closely by the earl, hurried to the back of the stage. Sure enough, lying senseless in the ditch, was the girl whom he had helped at the inn. Her gown and pelisse were covered in dust from the road, and her bonnet lay at an odd angle to her head. The cloakbag, which had been clutched tightly on her lap, had fallen a yard or two away.

The earl contemplated the still form in horror. A sour-faced man who had been sitting next to the girl leaned over the side. "She fell asleep, I think," he said as the earl, overcoming his dismay, dropped on one knee beside her. "I was awake, but I nearly fell off myself when we stopped."

"Well, you didn't, did you?" snapped the schoolboy, peering upwards.

"She ain't croaked, is she?" asked the coachman anxiously as he peered over his lordship's shoulder.

The earl got to his feet again, brushing a little

dust from the front of his coat. "No, she isn't dead," he answered, "but it looks as if she has knocked her head on that stone, and hit it quite badly." He continued to peer down at her and drew a small sigh. "There is only a small gash, but it may be serious. I think a physician should be called to attend her."

"A physician!" The coachman brought out a handkerchief and dabbed at his forehead. "I've got to bring this stage in on time, sir. I can't be waiting around here for the likes of one passenger, and an outside passenger at that."

In the short time since the unfortunate girl had been found, the other passengers of the stage had disembarked and were standing around staring down at the unconscious form with morbid curiosity.

"It must be obvious to you that she certainly cannot continue on her journey," retorted the earl, fast losing patience. "And she cannot remain here."

"And I've m'stage to bring in," repeated the driver.

"Poor little thing," murmured one lady traveller. "She be lying here in the dirt while you two argue. The gentleman is right; she needs a bed and a physician. Perhaps there's a farm where she can be taken. I've no intention of gettin' in agin 'til that poor lamb's taken care of."

A murmur of agreement passed round the other passengers and faced by this prospect of mutiny the driver's face grew red.

The earl drew a sigh of resignation. "Two of you fellows carry her to my carriage. My place is only half a mile from here. I shall have a physician brought from Leicester and when she is recovered she'll be sent on her way."

The coach driver looked reluctant and yet pleased at such a solution to this awkward problem. On seeing the uncertainty on the driver's face the earl added irritably, "My home is Glenbrooke Abbey." He drew out his card and pressed it on the man.

"It's no use, m'lord. I can't read."

He then handed the card to the sour-faced man who regarded it and its quality gravely and then nodded.

"I assure you on my word as a peer of the realm, I have no untoward intentions towards this girl."

The fat farmer, who had been watching the proceedings from the back of the crowd, now pushed his way forward. "Everyone could see him back at the inn filling her with flummery," he sneered. "How do we know he's who he says he is. His tongue is well hung, that's all we know of him."

At this insult Bracknell shook his fist in the man's face. "That's no mouthful o'moonshine my master's given you and if you dare say so again I'll put my fist down your throat!"

The two men faced each other fiercely for a moment or two before the coach driver said, "Oh, yer can see he's a real swell cove."

And the woman said, digging the farmer sharply in the ribs, "Don't yer know Quality when yer sees it?"

The earl walked away a few steps. "While you are arguing the pros and cons of my pedigree," he said quietly, "this poor child is lying in the dust. What is more, if you do not place her in my carriage immediately I shall make no more of it and you may do with her what you will."

So saying, the earl climbed into his curricle and a moment later Lucinda Kendricks was reverently placed beside him by the coach driver and Bracknell.

"See she is not jolted unduly, Bracknell," ordered his lordship.

Bracknell answered briskly, "Rely on me, m'lord," but he gave his master an odd sidelong glance which the earl did not miss.

As he flicked his whip lightly over the backs of his horses he too wondered why he had done something so quixotic as this. It was true the accident had been mainly his fault, if one discounted the recklessness by which the postchaise was being driven, and it was true there was nowhere else for her to be taken. It was also true that once at Glenbrooke Abbey the girl would be cared for by his many servants and he might never even see her again, but as he drove the curricle into the avenue leading to his magnificent Tudor mansion, he wondered if he were indeed turning soft in the head.

Chapter Two

Adeline Farringdon, Countess of Glenbrooke, saw her son driving up the avenue from the long gallery of Glenbrooke Abbey. For weeks now she had felt nothing but anger towards her elder child, and the fact that his valet and trunks had arrived hours ago did nothing to appease it. But at the sight of him approaching at last she could feel only great excitement and a good deal of delight.

She threw a paisley shawl over her black bombazine gown and hurried along the gallery and down the great staircase, crying to the footmen in the hall, "Your master is back! Isn't that wonderful!"

The footmen, whilst retaining their dignity, smiled slightly to themselves. The countess, although she invariably behaved in a way that would have brought a frown to the brow of her late husband—and often did—was respected by her servants. The earls of Glenbrooke were notorious for marrying women who were below their station. Usually it was to some merchant's daughter in order to replenish the estate coffers, sometimes it was for love, and occasionally for both. When Adeline had married Henry Farringdon she had brought him a very small portion, but a great deal of happiness which lasted until his premature death only a year before. The fact that she did not bring to her marriage great material riches did not stop her, or her late husband, or her son, enjoying every luxury and pursuit money could provide.

Without waiting for the butler to open the door, the countess flung it open and ran down the steps just as her son's curricle drew up outside.

"Dareth! Oh, darling, how marvellous it is to see you! I thought you would never come home."

The moment he stepped down she flung her arms around him. Good-naturedly he allowed his ever emotional mother to hug him for a few seconds and then he held her away.

"What a relief it is to have a welcome like this, Mother. I expected a scolding."

Having him here before her was so wonderful she just could not raise the anger his absence these past months had done.

"Oh, you naughty boy," she said reproachfully. "This past six months and more I have been preparing to welcome your bride to Glenbrooke Abbey."

His indulgent smile faded. "You have seen the *Gazette*, I take it?"

"I saw the announcement of Caroline Kingsley's

betrothal, if that is what you are meaning. I was expecting to see your name alongside hers, and what did I see instead? The Duke of Derwent's!"

"We shall discuss it later," he said, dismissing the subject abruptly.

She looked at him anxiously. "So we shall. But for now, have you eaten yet? You look a trifle hollow-eyed."

"Yes," he answered heavily, "I had dinner along the road."

Bracknell coughed discreetly and the earl turned round, recalling his unwelcome burden who still lay insensible in his curricle. "There is something more pressing I'm afraid."

As he moved the countess was able to see the girl for the first time. Her eyes widened in surprise and she gasped. "Good heavens!" She clapped her hands to her mouth, looking from one to the other, and then her eyes lit up. "Dareth! Oh, Dareth, you are married after all. I knew you would not return without a bride. Indeed, you knew you must not."

She waved the footmen forward. "Take the countess to the King's Bedchamber immediately, and be careful how you go."

After a moment's stunned silence the earl protested, "But, Mother, she isn't. . . ."

The countess in her excitement waved an impatient hand at him. "We'll talk later. Indeed we shall. But now we must get this poor child into bed." She shot him a scathing glance. "Thoughtless creature. Your father was just the same." Still taken aback at the unexpected turn of events, the earl watched as Lucinda was carried into the house. "The way you drive your team it's no wonder the child swooned."

"Mother...."

For once the warning note in his voice was completely ignored. She waved her hand at him again and hurried off after the solemn cortege.

His mother's impulsiveness was well known to everyone who was even mildly acquainted with her and usually it only managed to draw a smile from her son, but on this occasion he threw his whip down into the curricle in exasperation.

Bracknell, his expression bland, took the ribbons and the earl said quickly, in a somewhat preoccupied manner, "You'd better send Bradley straight away to fetch a physician."

"He'll have to go to Leicester, m'lord."

"Then send him there," the young man answered irritably and then as an after-thought, "and he can tell the fellow there'll be double the fee if he can be here within the hour."

The earl strode towards the house and then, as Bracknell was about to drive away, he turned back.

"And, Bracknell...."

The tiger looked blandly at his master. "Yes, m'lord?"

"Not a word about this ... matter until I have it straightened out."

Bracknell allowed himself a small smile. "Mum's the word, m'lord."

The earl sprinted up the steps and once inside the great hall with its stone floor, enormous fireplace and medieval tapestries, he allowed himself to be divested of his coat, hat and gloves.

"Welcome home, my lord," said Latimer, the butler.

The earl, his mind preoccupied, murmured an appropriate reply.

"And may I, on behalf of the others, my lord, be allowed the privilege of congratulating you?"

The earl let out a small sound of exasperation but was saved the embarrassment of replying by the appearance of his mother at the top of the staircase.

"Come along up, my love. We shall take tea in the drawing room." She glanced at the butler. "Tea, if you please, Latimer."

The earl looked at his butler. "Brandy, Latimer, for us both."

The butler's eyebrows rose a fraction but he simply answered, "As you wish, my lord."

The earl sprinted up the stairs. "She's quite comfortably settled in the King's Bedchamber," his mother said. "It seemed an occasion to use it. It's a shame for such a beautiful room to remain unused. I have always believed so. I doubt if we can expect a king to stay here now, so your wife may as well instead."

She laughed gaily as her son cupped her elbow

in his hand and led her towards the drawing room. "A physician should be here very shortly to attend her. I have sent Bradley to Leicester. Now, Mother, I must tell you. . . ."

As the earl led his mother into the room and closed the door behind them, her countenance fell. "Oh, is it really necessary to have a physician? But, I admit she does look an odd colour. Not used to travelling, I imagine."

"I wouldn't know," her son answered irritably, "simply because. . . ."

"Well, I have left her in good hands. My own dear Fraser is attending her and will do so, I promise, until her own maid arrives." She smiled foolishly. "You are a naughty boy for not letting me know about this, although it is such an agreeable surprise I cannot admit to being angry. Oh, by the way, what is her name?"

"I've no idea," answered the earl with a slight shrug of his broad shoulders, having some time ago given up trying to break into her excited chatter.

"You don't know," echoed his mother.

Their conversation was interrupted by the arrival of Latimer and the brandy. When he had been dismissed by his master, the earl poured the liquid into two glasses and handed one to his mother.

"Did I hear you say you didn't know her name?" insisted her ladyship. "Are you funning, Dareth? If so I abhor your humour."

"The truth is, Mother, I have never clapped

eyes on the girl before this very afternoon. I cannot understand what gave you the idea that she could be my wife!"

The countess looked outraged. "Oh, surely you cannot have brought one of your. . . ."

"No I haven't," the earl answered quickly, "and you know full well I never would. The truth of the matter is, the stagecoach had a slight accident almost outside the gates of Glenbrooke Abbey, and I simply had no choice but to bring the girl here. She was travelling alone and there was nowhere else for her to go. I could hardly leave her lying in the road," he added, wishing now that he had done just that.

To his dismay his mother's eyes filled with tears. She stumbled her way to a sofa which stood before the fire and sank down into it. For a moment she stared unseeingly into the flames and then, remembering the glass in her hand, she drained it quickly.

"Then you are not, after all, married."

"No," he answered gently.

She held out the glass without looking at him. He refilled it for her and after handing it back, sat down beside her and took her free hand in his.

"Do you really think I would arrive in such a manner with my *wife*?"

His mother's eyes were filled with tears. She shook her head. "I was so disappointed when I heard of Miss Kingsley's engagement, and then, when I saw this girl, I just thought. . . ."

"The trouble is," her son said gently, "you *never* think, Mother. Is it likely I would bring home so shabby a bride?"

His mother's gaze remained fixed on the fire. "I noticed only that she had the sweetest countenance."

"She is some unfortunate girl whose circumstances force her to travel alone and on the outside. Is your brain so fuddled over this matter that you would match me with her?"

She levelled her blue eyes at him then. "I would have you married to anyone rather than see Uncle Percival's wealth go to a foundling hospital."

The earl let out a gasp of exasperation and sank back into the cushions. "That would be a very high price to pay for Great Uncle Percival's fortune."

He got to his feet and walked across to the window which overlooked extensive parkland. Deer roamed and grazed contentedly beyond the ditch which prevented them from coming close to the house.

He gazed out for a few moments and when his mother said, "I cannot conceive why Caroline Kingsley rejected your offer, Dareth," the earl turned to face her again.

"I don't believe she did." His mother turned to look at him quizzically. "It was," he explained, "her father who preferred the Duke of Derwent, I am convinced of it."

"But why? He always received you most civilly."

"Yes, he did, but I dare say," her son answered mildly, "a rumour that we are not so affluent as we once were, has reached his ears."

"And so Caroline refused you and accepted that bloodless stick."

The earl laughed. "Precisely."

His mother looked indignant. "It is no matter for levity, my dear. She must surely prefer you, Dareth."

"I'm sure she does."

The countess made a most unladylike snort of derision and then said, "Perhaps it's just as well she did refuse you. If she is so meek as to accept her father's dictates rather than that of her heart, then I shouldn't want her as your wife. But," she added with a sigh, "it would have been wonderful having her portion in addition to the forty thousand pounds wedding gift Uncle Percival promised."

"May as well not think about it," said her son philosophically.

"I have done nothing *but* think about it for months."

"You've probably done nothing but think about how the money was to have been spent."

"There's certainly a great deal we could do with it," she murmured thoughtfully, and then, "It's too bad, Dareth. You said you had a mind to marry Caroline. You should have pressed your suit more forcefully."

The earl looked no more than mildly surprised. "I assure you I flattered her unendingly, but perhaps a little less than the Duke of Derwent. Are you suggesting we should have eloped in defiance of her father? Miss Kingsley was not averse to Derwent. He was forever flattering the silly chit."

"You might have done something more than you did. You admitted a liking for the chit and you certainly knew what was at stake. I refuse to believe that a man of your address could not make *any* woman fall in love with you. I know it to be a fact, Dareth. I have watched the young girls fall for you in droves. Only in the past you have been spoiled by their adoration, and choosing a wife has never been a matter of such urgency. You chose too late. That is the trouble. You were too sure of your reception."

The earl drew out his watch and after glancing at it briefly said as he put it away, "Well, it's as you said, Mother, it wouldn't have done at all. She has no spirit. A biddable wife would be delightful for a while, but a bore before very long."

The countess gave another gasp of exasperation and wagged one finger at her son. "When you should have been pursuing Miss Kingsley these past weeks, you've been keeping company with that lightskirt, admit it."

"If you allude to Mrs Cartwright, Mother, I don't deny it," he answered easily. "I find her company invigorating. But it has nothing to do with my relationship with Miss Kingsley. The actual reason for my delay in returning was an extremely interesting mill at Flaxton between Charley...."

His mother held up her hand. "I don't wish to know. You are quite incorrigible, Dareth. Your pleasures must always come first even when something as important as a fortune is at stake."

"But it isn't, Mother," he reminded her. "I am now one week off thirty, and I am not married. I have lost the wedding gift and the inheritance that might have been mine."

The countess fell back upon the cushions. Her body went almost completely limp. "It's just too much to bear," she murmured. "You talk of it as easily as you would a lost wager at White's. I was so sure that a man so handsome and of such good stock, one who has set so many female hearts racing...." Her son smiled slightly. "... must surely find himself a bride within the stipulated period."

His eyes twinkled. "Oh, I most assuredly could, but," he added as his mother raised her head feebly, "just as surely you would not have approved or accepted any of them."

Her ladyship drew away from him and got abruptly to her feet. "I despair of you, Dareth. My only consolation is that your father and his father were rakes of the first order until they married. *If* you ever do...."

His face still bore an expression of amusement. "Surely you would not have me marry *anyone*?"

The countess arranged her shawl about her shoulders. "Naturally I would prefer someone of rank and fortune. In fact, from now on, Dareth, seeing you do not have one of your own, it will definitely have to be someone of fortune."

"Even if she has the face of a hag?" the earl teased.

"You will never marry anyone of that description. Quite the contrary," she sighed. "You have the sort of disposition to marry a penniless beauty just for love."

"Like Father?"

Her eyes grew soft and misty. "Precisely." She put her hand on his arm and he said gently, "Do you still miss him?"

"More than anyone will ever know," she answered dreamily, and then added briskly, "but he would not want me to grieve for ever, not outwardly anyway. And as long as I have you, I can bear it because you are so much like him in every way."

She moved away again. "Not Melissa, of course. She favours my aunt, Matilda, poor child.

Dareth laughed and his mother said, "And now what are we to do with that girl upstairs?"

His smile faded. "It couldn't have happened at a worse time."

She clapped her hand to her forehead. "I forgot to tell you, Uncle Percival will be arriving some time tomorrow." The earl groaned. "I felt sure you must at least come home affianced if not actually married. That was why I was so anxious for your arrival."

He smiled then. "How odd. I thought you were glad to see me for my own sake."

"Silly boy," she chided, "you know I was." She sighed then. "But it chased the matter out of my mind when I saw that girl in your curricle."

"Then perhaps it is just as well I brought her."

His mother opened her mouth to say something more when the butler came in to announce the arrival of the physician.

"He's taken a deuce of a time to get here."

"Oh, I'm sure the matter isn't all that urgent," said the countess, moving towards the door. "I'll accompany him and let you know his verdict. I'm sure there is no need for alarm."

When she had gone the room seemed unnaturally quiet. The earl remained where he was, in the centre of the room, staring at the closed door. Now he was alone his face took on an expression of severity. By now, having overheard his mother's rash words, the whole houseful of servants would think he had arrived with his wife; in another hour the whole estate would know. His problem now was how to explain away his "wife."

"She's still out of her senses!" exclaimed the countess the very next morning as she burst breathlessly into the breakfast room.

Her son who had been staring morosely into his

coffee cup looked up sharply. "Are you sure she's *still* unconscious?"

His mother's arrival had broken into his thoughts in the most unwelcome way. Although he humoured his mother and pretended he did not care, the refusal of Caroline Kingsley to accept his offer of marriage had hurt him sorely. He had reached an age where he wished for the delights of matrimony, and a family to brighten his old age. Since his sister's marriage both Glenbrooke Abbey and the Grosvenor Square house seemed empty and lifeless.

This had nothing to do whatsoever with Great Uncle Percival's stipulation that his heir should be married before he reached the age of thirty, or the money would go to a foundling hospital. Not that the money wasn't important; it was. The earls of Glenbrooke and their families had always lived beyond their means and, Dareth supposed, always would.

"She hasn't stirred a muscle since she was laid in the bed yesterday evening." She sank down into a chair and reached for a piece of toast. "I don't think I could touch anything else this morning. I am quite perturbed. I thought she would regain her senses within a very short time."

"So did I," answered her son as he stared into space. He looked up at his mother. "When does the physician call again?"

"This afternoon."

He pushed away his cup. He too had had very

little appetite for food. "You are right," he said abruptly. "This sounds as if it might be a serious matter."

The countess bit into her toast. "No, no. I don't think so. At least Dr Bishop seems unconcerned."

"He is a country quack and did not impress me with his learning."

"Yet you paid him double the fee."

"It was promised." He leaned forward slightly. "This is, frankly, Mother, very worrying."

His mother gave a harsh laugh. "More worrying for poor Miss Kendricks, I should say."

"And whom might she be?" asked the earl who, though used to his mother's vagaries was nevertheless irritated by them from time to time.

The countess paused wide-eyed as she helped herself to another slice of toast. "The victim of the accident." She buttered the slice carefully and then looked up at her son who was cast into deep thought once more. "Pour me some coffee, darling, if you will."

He did so and then as he placed the pot back on its stand, "I have taken responsibility for this girl and it would be rather unfortunate if she were to die in my care. The gossips need much less to label it more than a tragic accident."

His mother flushed slightly. "Oh, there is no chance of that, is there? Dr Bishop was very hopeful of her complete recovery. He doubted if there was any damage at all to her brain, although naturally he couldn't be sure."

"Naturally," said the earl drily. "She may remain unconscious permanently. I have heard of such cases."

"Oh, don't say so, my love, or you will cast me into the dismals too. It would be too much like the sleeping beauty of the fairy tale."

The earl laughed then. "And who should we have as the prince?"

His mother pretended to consider for a moment or two. "Why not Digby Stacey?" she suggested, naming her daughter's brother-in-law whom both the earl and his mother held in dislike.

"I don't know Miss Kendricks at all, but I'm sure she wouldn't like to be wakened by such a deadly bore as he. Besides, is he not in the Peninsula with Wellesley's men?"

"Was," answered his mother, whose mouth was filled with toast at that moment. "He caught some shot in the leg at Talavera. He's still convalescing, poor man. Melissa tells me that if Sir Arthur himself hadn't insisted his own physician attend Lieutenant Stacey, the leg might have been lost."

The earl's eyes gleamed. "They'll make a man of him yet." His smile faltered. "We must be serious, Mother...."

"By all means do, dear," she answered, showing an unconcern which was beginning to irritate him anew.

"If this girl's condition isn't worrying enough, I am at a loss as to how I am going to explain my not being married to her after all. You do realise that the news will have spread by now? There were too many who heard to stop it doing so."

The countess gave a little giggle. "Oh, I shouldn't worry so on that score. Everyone expects the Farringdons to act outrageously. We always have been a reckless breed. Your being respectably married is more likely to set the county alight with wonder."

Dareth gazed across at his mother. With her eyes alive with laughter, in her mauve muslin dress, her hair fashionably cropped and curling about her head, she looked no older than the girls he paid court to, and he could not find it in him to be angry at her outrageousness, nor the way she shrugged off so characteristically the problem which had caused him a sleepless night.

"I can see that it is useless even to discuss it with you, Mother. Any answer will have to be found by me alone. As usual you refuse to help at all."

"It will all come right," she said, giving a philosophical shrug as her son shook his head sadly, although he could not help but smile. "I hope you're not going far today," she said a moment later. "I should like you to be around when your great uncle arrives."

Dareth smiled tightly. "I shall only be exercising my horses this morning. I shall be here to greet him, but don't suppose I will toady to him, Mother."

The countess looked outraged. "As if I would expect such a thing of you!"

The earl leaned back in his chair and selected a rosy apple from the dish. "You know," he said, regarding his mother carefully, "the answer to all this is for you to marry a man who is able to support you in the style you enjoy so much."

His mother, who at first looked astonished, then laughed. "Oh really! And whom, may I ask, have you in mind? I do assume you have someone in mind, or will any rich old man do?"

"Sir Richard Crosbie."

The countess let out a hoot of laughter. "Poor Dickie. He did say, when I married your father, that if he couldn't have me for his wife he would never marry—and he never has—but I doubt if he would want me now."

"I disagree." The earl bit into the apple with deliberation. "He is never far from your side for long, remember, and never has been for as far back as I can recall. As a child I always believed it was his interest in me as his god-son that brought him to our house so often. As I grew older I grew wiser too."

"Well, be that as it may, Dareth, and I don't deny it, it certainly does not help *you*. You are entitled to Uncle Percival's fortune, being his only heir."

"But I am not going to get it, am I, unless I marry by the end of next week, which I assure you I shall not do."

She wrung her hands in sudden anguish and then, picking up the coffee pot, thrust it at a footman who was standing behind her chair. "More coffee, if you please." She turned back to her son. "I'm infuriated to think about it! That vulgar old man whose money should be yours by right, making conditions if you please."

"You were not outraged when it appeared I would be married in time."

She chose to ignore his last remark and asked, "Where is his gratitude? A family of middle class merchants, that is all they really are. Your grandfather made his sister a countess."

"For a considerable portion."

"I really don't know how we are to explain away Miss Kendricks to him."

"Why trouble?"

But by now the countess was in no mood to listen. Her eyes were agleam with a sudden excitement. "Dareth, you have just given me the most wonderful idea!"

Her son's laughter turned into a groan. "Heaven forbid."

"I am being serious."

"Never."

She dimpled. "It's quite simple. You intend to be married one day, don't you, dear?"

"Certainly."

"Then why not pretend you are now."

"And my wife?"

"Miss Kendricks, of course."

He laughed again. "Oh, no, my love, we're not getting tangled up in that kind of deceit."

"Just a business arrangement, of course, Dareth, and it would be just for the duration of Uncle Percival's visit. Not a minute longer, I promise."

He looked upwards. "Won't Miss Kendricks have words to say about that?"

"Oh, why can't you be serious for a moment?"

"I'm trying to be, Mother," he said, laughing again, "but you make it exceedingly difficult."

"Once she is recovered, and it could be at any moment, we shall put the proposition to her."

"She will not agree. No woman in her right sense would."

"For fifty guineas she will not hesitate."

The earl drew an almost imperceptible sigh. "Oh, I see. Well, she won't do it. And by the look of her she is not even equipped to do it. Even Great Uncle Percival will see she's a raw girl quite beyond her station. He knows me better than that, don't you believe otherwise. And her family won't allow it even if she and I were foolish enough to agree on such a lunatic course."

Much to his consternation she fumbled in the bodice of her gown and drew out two letters. "She has no family, Dareth. She's an orphan, poor child." Her eyes suddenly filled with tears. "I cannot help but compare her unfortunate situation in life to that of my darling Melissa."

She drew a sigh and said, dabbing away the tears, "There are two letters here, both of them of introduction. She's going into service in the household of a Mrs Purvey." The countess waved the letters in the air. "She's probably the wife of a cloth merchant. Even so, I suppose I should write a note to assure her Miss Kendricks is in good hands, although I doubt if she really would care."

The earl eyed his mother steadily. "When Miss Kendricks is sufficiently recovered to continue her journey we shall see she is put safely on the earliest stage."

"What kind of a woman can she be who allows a child—she is no more than that—to be an outside traveller? I shudder to think of it."

"It does not concern us," answered her son mildly, placing the apple core on his plate.

"Oh, please, Dareth," she begged, fearing that he was about to leave her. "We have spent enormously these past few years and I don't have to tell you how much it cost to have Melissa settled so comfortably. We will be helping the girl too. Fifty guineas is far more than she will see in a whole lifetime of service, and to me it isn't even the price of a new gown and to you the most meagre of bets."

"No, Mother," he answered. "Even if it were possible for Miss Kendricks to go along with such a hoax, you seem to forget that we shall have to answer to Great Uncle Percival for good, not just for the duration of his visit here. I cannot have a wife during his stay and not afterwards. It doesn't make sense, even for you."

"La! As if that matters. Uncle Percival has lived in Bath for the past thirty years—ever since it became unfashionable, which is typical of him. He never reads a journal, nor does he socialise to any extent. His only visitors are rustics who know nothing of the London social scene."

"I shouldn't underestimate what Great Uncle Percival learns about us, Mother."

"But he is over eighty now and not in the best of health, sad to say. He cannot live much longer."

Her son let out a shout of laughter. "You have been singing that same tune since I was on leading-strings, Mother. If you want my opinion, I believe Great Uncle Percival will outlive us all." He got to his feet. "I'd best be going now, if I am to return in time to pay my respects to the old fellow when he arrives. Mind you," he teased, "I could always show him the door. There's no point in toadying to him any more."

His mother drew herself up indignantly. "You cannot possibly be serious. Where is your sense of family, Dareth? I still live in hope that his conscience will not allow him to disinherit you and that his mind can be changed." She looked up at him hopefully. "It was a very good idea, my love."

The earl leaned across the table and eyed his mother steadily. "I absolutely forbid it, Mother." He turned to go, ignoring the pleading look in her eyes. He walked as far as the door and as the footman opened it he looked at her again. "A deception of that kind is out of the question."

Chapter Three

The countess stood at the head of the stairs as the doctor came towards her. Dareth was out still, and she had spent much of the afternoon waiting for the arrival of Percival Courtney-Smythe. Her mind continued to work endlessly, but it was to no avail. The problem uppermost in her mind—apart from the loss of her son's inheritance—was how to explain away Lucinda Kendricks' presence.

She was well aware of the reason her late husband's uncle had insisted that, to benefit, Dareth should be married by the time he reached the age of thirty. Percival Courtney-Smythe was of a sober disposition and he always disapproved of the pleasure-seeking ways of the Farringdons. The presence of a young girl, unconscious, at the Abbey would not serve to change his mind.

The physician bowed low before her. "Ah, doctor!" she cried. regaining some of her usual gaiety. "What a relief it is to see you!"

"How is my patient?" he asked after taking the countess's proferred hand momentarily. His face, with sagging folds of flesh, reminded the countess of her son's retrievers. The doctor had a permanent hopeful, yet mournful, expression on his face, which was unfortunate to one of his calling.

She began to escort him along the gallery towards the bedrooms. She has been restless for the past two or three hours. "My own personal maid-servant has not left her side. We have waited for your arrival most anxiously."

The physician frowned thoughtfully. "It sounds very much as though she will soon be conscious. I think we may see some developments in her condition very soon."

The countess clasped her hands together. "Oh, do you think so, doctor?" She was wondering if it were at all possible to have the girl out of the house by the time the old man arrived. It was a very doubtful possibility, even to the countess to whom nothing seemed impossible. "I do hope you may be right," and added in a characteristically exaggerated manner, "My son is quite beside himself with worry."

The doctor allowed himself a small smile which did nothing to relieve his hang-dog expression. "I don't believe there is sufficient cause for that, my lady. I have known several cases where the patient has been insensible for far longer periods of time, and suffered no untoward consequences afterwards because of it."

"I do hope you may be right," she repeated, not entirely convinced, as they came to the door of the King's Bedchamber.

Rarely having a serious thought in her head, the countess was now realising that Dareth had a basis for his fears; it would be extremely embarrassing if the girl were to die under their roof.

Fraser, who had been in the service of the countess for more than forty years, was sitting by the bed. When her mistress ushered the doctor inside she put down her sewing and, jumping to her feet, dropped a little curtsey.

The room was the largest in the house, its Tudor-style furnishings unchanged since the wife of Jeremiah Farringdon had chosen them. The only recent additions were the Turkish rugs to temper the chillness of bare wooden floors.

Lucinda Kendricks for the first time in her life lay on a bed fit for a king. It was a specially constructed four-poster, large enough to accommodate King Henry the Eighth in his later years when his body was immense. Never was it intended to accommodate so slight a figure as Lucinda.

The moment they entered the room the countess asked, for the tenth time that day, "How is she, Fraser?"

"Restless, my lady; more than before I should say."

The doctor walked up to the impressive bed and pulled back the hangings which were of the finest

French tapestry, depicting King Henry's coat of arms and flattering scenes from his life.

"Ah, her colour is much better. I can see that immediately. Yes, and her pulse is steady too. Most satisfactory."

The countess remained at the other side of the bed, wringing her hands together in anguish. "But when can we expect her to awake?"

The doctor leaned further over his restless patient. "At any moment, I should say." He shook Lucinda's arm. "Come along, my dear, wake up now. You have slept for long enough."

"I don't think that. . . ." the countess began to protest but just at that moment Lucinda opened her eyes and stared blankly at the man bending over her.

"This is much better," said the doctor. "Very much better. How do you feel, my dear? Better, eh?"

"My head," she murmured, moving it restlessly. "My head aches."

The doctor chuckled. "And so it will for quite some time. But not to worry, my dear. The ache *will* go."

The countess gazed at Lucinda anxiously as the girl looked around her, her eyes wide with bewilderment.

"Your family are most concerned for you," added the doctor.

"My family?" asked the girl, frowning.

As Lucinda continued to look about her, the

countess drew her anxious gaze away. "We're not. . . ." she began to say, but again was not allowed to finish.

Her attention was once more claimed by the patient who asked, "What happened to me?" Her face was still, understandably, a picture of bewilderment.

"There was an accident," answered the countess in her gentlest voice, "between the curricle belonging to my son and the stagecoach. Do you not remember?"

Lucinda shook her head. "I remember nothing."

The doctor looked across to the countess. "This is not unknown in such cases. Occasionally a patient cannot recall the circumstances immediately before and during the accident. The memory of it will probably return gradually." As the countess slowly nodded her understanding he looked down at his patient again. "Tell me the last thing you do remember, my dear."

Lucinda plucked nervously at the top sheet. "I cannot tell you anything at all," she said, frowning again.

"Come now," urged the doctor, still using his cheerful tone, which was beginning to annoy the countess. "You must recall something."

"No! Nothing. I don't even know where I am. I've never been in this room before."

"That's true," answered the countess, beginning to feel a little alarmed at the girl's obvious distress. "You have never been here before."

"Where?"

"Glenbrooke Abbey."

"I've never heard of it. Who are you?"

The doctor gasped at so outrageous a question. Everyone must surely know the Countess of Glenbrooke, renowned throughout the fashionable world for her sweetness and beauty.

But the countess herself simply smiled and answered, "I am Adeline, Countess of Glenbrooke."

Lucinda looked away. "I am sorry," she murmured. "I should have known."

"No," answered the countess, "we have never met before."

The girl struggled to sit up. "Then why am I here?"

"Can't you recall?" asked the doctor.

"No!" answered the girl in anguish as the countess looked beseechingly at the doctor.

"What is the matter with her?" she asked, fast becoming as perplexed as the girl.

"I can't remember at all." She put one hand to her head, her eyes opening wide in horror. She looked from the doctor to the countess. "I don't even know who I am!"

There was a full minute of silence, punctuated only by the sound of a sob issuing from Fraser's lips. The countess stepped back as if stung and the doctor's jaw dropped open.

Lucinda looked at the countess, her green eyes filled with immeasurable pain. She reached out and touched her arm. "Who am I and what am I doing here? Please, I beg of you, tell me!"

The countess swallowed the lump in her throat and gave the doctor a look of mute appeal, but none of his learning could help a situation such as this. He made a nervous adjustment to his wig and swallowed noisily as he said, "Pray tell her, my lady."

The countess stared at him for a moment or two. Her heart was beating loudly beneath her ribs. Then she asked in a very deliberate voice, "Do you not remember travelling from London?"

The girl shook her head. "Please, tell me who I am. I remember nothing."

The countess drew herself up straight. "You are my son's wife—the new Countess of Glenbrooke."

"My God, Mother! What made you do it?"

Dareth leaned his forehead against the cool pane of one of the drawing room windows in an attempt to check the fever of fury that was raging inside him.

His mother twisted a lace-edged handkerchief in her hands. "She just didn't know who she was and how she came to be here, and I realised no one here, apart from our two selves, did either. Oh, please don't be angry with me, dearest. It was done for your sake as much as mine; more so, in fact."

He whirled round. He was still wearing his riding clothes. "I don't doubt your intentions, Mother," he said in a carefully controlled voice, but the fury was plainly to be seen in his eyes. Although it had, in the past, rarely been directed towards her, his mother recognised it all too well.

"After I forbade you only this morning, I cannot credit you with such foolishness."

"But matters have changed, Dareth, since this morning."

"I cannot see that." Indignantly he brought out his snuff box and took a pinch between his thumb and forefinger.

"Only think, my love. I realise now that my earlier scheme *was*, I admit, foolhardy." Her son allowed himself a grim smile. "We would have been too much reliant upon Miss Kendricks' acting ability, which now I realise could not be too great. But no longer are we reliant upon that. She will believe whatever we tell her!"

She stared hopefully at his uncompromising expression for a moment or two and then said in exasperation, "But it's Providence, Dareth, that she should come to us just at this time. Surely you must own I am right."

He continued to regard her severely. "There is nothing right about it. My problem now is how to explain away such a monstrous 'mistake.' The whole county must be by now preparing to call on the bride!"

His mother gave a little gasp of dismay and then a devilish smile lit up her son's face. "Perhaps I could persuade everyone," he mused, "that you are hopelessly insane." She gasped again and he continued, waving one finger in her astonished face. "Yes, I am convinced that is the answer. It will also have the double effect of answering any future blunder you may make."

Her eyes filled with tears. "Oh, how cruel you are, Dareth. I don't know where you have got such a cruel streak. The Farringdons for all their faults were never cruel, neither were any of my family."

"The first earl, I believe, could lay claim to a bestial nature," he answered, quite unmoved by her distress. "And I am a direct decendant."

Suddenly the tears in her eyes spilled over on to her cheeks. "I shall kill myself," she vowed, "to save you embarrassment."

He smiled, albeit tightly. "That would cause me no end of embarrassment, Mother, so set that course from your mind immediately."

She flung herself face downwards into the cushions of the sofa, sobbing heartbrokenly. Tears had always been her best weapon; they had never failed to move her late husband. And like the best soldiers she did not use such drastic tactics often, thus ensuring their effectiveness in the field of battle. Like his father before him, the earl was unable to withstand such an onslaught on his senses. Her tears never failed to soften his resolve either. He went across the room and, sitting on the edge of the sofa, he took the forlorn figure in his arms. He held her close until the tears began to abate, and anyone coming in on the scene would have been forgiven for believing it were father and daughter in such an embrace, instead of mother and son.

"Oh, my dearest boy," she sobbed, "my thoughts are only for you. Only think what you could do with a gift of forty thousand pounds, not to mention what he will leave you in his will."

"I could," he agreed, "do a great deal with such a sum, but I could not accept it dishonestly, and if you would take time to examine your own conscience neither would you allow it."

She drew away from him. "It would not be dishonest!" She dabbed daintily at her eyes. "Oh, what a sight I must look. Uncle Percival will know immediately that something is wrong."

There was a light in her son's eyes she did not like. "If not immediately, Mother, very soon after."

"Dareth, how can it be dishonest? It isn't your fault you're not married. You couldn't know Caroline would refuse you. She gave you every reason to believe she would accept your offer. It *isn't* your fault."

"I'm afraid it is. I didn't press my suit as passionately as I should have done, and that's the truth of the matter."

The countess threw up her hands in a grand gesture of despair. "You intend to marry," she reasoned. "What difference does it make if it is now or next year?"

"A great deal to Great Uncle Percival."

"Oh, you are so noble, Dareth! Do you know why we are perpetually short of funds?"

Her son looked mildly surprised. He sat back into the corner of the sofa. "Because we enjoy our pleasures so . . . generously."

The countess gave one of her usual gasps of exasperation. "So do most of our friends and acquaintances, Dareth, and many of them have less acreage and far less property than we." She leaned closer. "We may take our pleasures seriously but we Farringdons also take our responsibilities seriously too. As far back as I can recall your father—and you are following him exactly—put almost as much into the estate as he took out."

"That is how it should be."

"Of course, but your great uncle only knows about the money spent on idle pursuits. He doesn't look to see what a good landlord you are, the miserable toad."

He laughed and she added indignantly, "He thinks that by making you wed he'd have you shackled to a shrew who will curtail all your frollicking. As if you would choose a harridan, and in any event as if you would allow marriage to curtail your activities." She paused to draw breath. "As if marriage made any difference to your father's life or mine in that respect."

He laughed again. "I've never seen a happier pair than you two, and you survived without Great Uncle Percival's money. I shall manage too."

She was about to voice an argument but for once he was able to forestall her. He leaned forward and caught her hands in his. "We shall have to cut down spending; that is all it means. You will have to manage with the gowns you already have for a while. . . ."

"Oh, Dareth."

"And I shall stay at home and stop gambling. . . ."

"You'd hate that."

"No, I wouldn't. I shall enjoy being the master of my own household in the fullest sense of the word. London is beginning to bore me anyway. We are not penniless, you know, just a little low in funds."

"What shall we do about Miss Kendricks?"

His face darkened. "Now, that is a problem, isn't it? She'll be preening herself right at this moment, imagining herself the Countess of Glenbrooke."

"No, she isn't. I don't think she's at all pleased to be a countess. She's thoroughly confused, poor child."

"And no wonder!"

The countess looked at him hopefully. "Couldn't we. . . ?"

"No!"

She sighed and sank back into the sofa's cushions. "It was such a good scheme, and her arrival was so opportune."

"I don't think you've thought out all the problems that could arise from such a madcap idea.

What will Mrs Purvey do, for instance, when her servant," he deliberately stressed this word, "fails to arrive?"

His mother remained silent for a minute or two and then said triumphantly, "I've already dispatched a note informing her of the accident. All I have to do is follow it up with a note saying that Miss Kendricks is dead! There will be no further enquiries, I guarantee."

The earl smiled wryly and shook his head. "I believe you would do it, too."

His mother bridled. "Of course I would. There is a great deal at stake."

"My sanity."

The countess drew the letters from the bodice of her dress again, becoming indignant anew. "You needn't think she is entirely unworthy of you. It says here in one of the letters, from the matron of this asylum which has harboured the poor girl since she was ... Dareth, you are not listening to me."

He had been drumming his fingers impatiently on the arm of the sofa and gazing indolently around the room. Now he returned his attention to his mother and said in the mildest of tones, "Be assured that I am, Mother."

She settled back once more. "Her father was a Lieutenant Theodore Kendricks of the Royal Navy. He fell at the battle of the Nile, quite heroically, may I add. Lucinda's mother grew consumptive and when she knew she was dying she used what little money she had to ensure her daughter's place in this establishment because the lieutenant had married beneath his station and the Kendricks family would not take her." She perused the letter thoughtfully. "I must say it seems a very enlightened type of establishment." She looked at her son. "I once knew a man named Kendricks who I believe did go into the navy. He was quite, quite charming." She smiled at so pleasant a memory, adding, "I wonder if it can be the same man."

"I doubt it," her son answered, "but I am glad for Miss Kendricks' sake that her antecedents are so respectable. Have you informed her of these facts?"

The countess flushed. "Some of them, certainly. I didn't, of course, mention the asylum. I told her she had been living. . . ." She hesitated. ". . . with an aunt in Hampstead."

"Poor Miss Kendricks," he said shortly. "I do believe she was better placed at the orphan asylum."

His mother laughed nervously and then her laughter died at the sight of his worried frown. "Indeed, I am sorry, Dareth. I have caused you unnecessary anguish."

He thumped his fist down on the arm of the sofa as he stared fiercely into the fire. "I'm dashed if I know how you thought you could carry it off. The girl looks as poor as a church mouse. My guess is that she only had a change of linen in that

cloakbag of hers, and the gown she was wearing
... well...."

"Oh, that is easily settled," said his mother with
a gay laugh. "I had her put into one of my best
bedgowns immediately, and as for her other
clothes, she is much the same size as Melissa. She
could wear her gowns and even if they are two
years out of date, no one here will notice."

He looked at his mother with a pair of eyes that
had set many a female heart fluttering. "If I am
not being a trifle naive," he said languidly, "what
are Melissa's clothes doing here when her home is
now at Stockley Hall? Do I dare to hope she has
come to her senses at last and left that pompous ass
she saw fit to marry in what I can only assume
was one of her more lightheaded moments?"

The countess laughed delightedly. "He is pompous, isn't he? But rich, Dareth. Very, very rich.
And in the last letter I received from your sister
she did nothing but praise Hugo. They are extremely happy. And I do wish you would try to
like your brother-in-law. Hugo may not be a Corinthian, but he really is a goodnatured fellow."

"That," replied her son emphatically, "is what
I dislike about him most. And you still haven't
told me why Melissa is running around Stockley
Hall in her petticoats."

"Silly boy. She is doing nothing of the kind, as
you well know. Naturally, when Melissa became
betrothed we purchased an entirely new wardrobe

of clothes. She could not come to her husband as a dowd!"

"You may consider me a fool for asking." He drew out his watch and glanced at it. "I wonder when the old boy will arrive. I had better change in readiness for dinner."

At the mention of Uncle Percival the countess's expression grew woeful. Her son got to his feet and replaced his watch in his waistcoat pocket. She began to pick at her handkerchief.

"What *are* we to tell him?"

"The truth, of course," her son answered promptly with an expression of only the mildest surprise.

"I shall look such a fool in front of the servants."

"I dare say you will," he said, and added drily, "but being servants they don't signify."

She pulled at the handkerchief until the lace began to come away at the edge. "What am I to tell Miss Kendricks?"

"Exactly that. She *is* Miss Kendricks. Unless, of course, you wish me to have you declared insane. That will relieve you of all responsibility."

"Heartless child," she murmured.

"And perhaps the day after tomorrow Bradley or Bracknell will drive her to the inn in time to catch the stage." He leaned forward slightly, lowering his voice. "I shall even purchase a ticket for her to continue the journey inside the coach."

The countess refused to be impressed by so generous an offer. She simply continued to stare at the floor, her face a picture of unrelieved misery.

The earl stood with his back to the fire, his hands clasped behind his back. "I really am surprised at you, Mama." She rallied a little at the use of so fond a name. "You have given no thought to poor Miss Kendricks and her feelings in this matter."

"But I have. She will love being a countess. What girl would not?"

His eyebrows rose a fraction. "In her condition she will truly believe it is so, unless, of course, her memory returns during Great Uncle Percival's visit. . . ."

The countess considered for a moment. "Dr Bishop doubts that it will return so soon."

"What does he know of such matters?"

"He is a trained physician."

The earl was unimpressed. "No one knows about the workings of the brain and no one ever will. She may never remember, in which case we may never be rid of her."

"You are trying to frighten me."

"Yes."

"Oh, really, this is all supposition. Great Uncle Percival never stays longer than a se'ennight before he begins to contemplate the long journey home and decides to have it done with as soon as possible. It is always the case. And as I have already said he is not a young man, nor is he robust. Only a year ago he suffered a severe illness which prevented him from attending your father's funeral. He has come only now to gloat over your bachelorhood."

Dareth laughed shortly. "I really feel he should be congratulating me."

"And as for her never remembering, it is most unlikely."

"Well, just suppose it went according to your crazy plan and Great Uncle Percival, who is no one's fool, was persuaded to believe that . . . chit is my chosen wife, and Miss Kendricks comes to no emotional harm through such a pretence, she will have lost her position with Mrs. . . ." He waved his hand impatiently in the air.

"Purvey," his mother supplied. "As to that, I'm not at all convinced she is a good mistress. I'm not convinced at all. I could find her a much better position and give her a testimonial no one could question. You really do underestimate your mother, Dareth."

He smiled fondly. "Not at all, my love, and that is why I'm quaking.

"Besides, this is all supposition. It is most unlikely that Miss Kendricks will conveniently remain without her memory until Great Uncle Percival leaves, and then meekly accept any position you may find for her. She would be quite entitled to insist on remaining here as my wife, at least whilst my great uncle lives. We may be at the mercy of a woman more unscrupulous than you."

"That is absolute nonsense, Dareth! The girl is quite an innocent. A fool could see that."

He smiled slightly. "And let no one call you that."

"You are mocking me, Dareth," she complained, turning away from him.

"Well, I shall leave you to inform Miss Kendricks, as you will, of her true identity." He hurried across the room. "Great Uncle Percival will be here for dinner after all," he said when he reached the window, and then, turning to his mother, asked mildly, "Shall we go to greet him?"

Chapter Four

The countess stood at the top of the steps tensely clasping her hands before her as she awaited the arrival of Percival Courtney-Smythe's ancient, but nonetheless elegant, equipage. When it stopped, the earl hurried down the steps to greet his great uncle who emerged, with a great deal of wheezing, from the carriage, assisted by two footmen.

"Welcome to Glenbrooke Abbey, Great Uncle Percival," said the earl, bestowing upon him a more cordial smile than might have been expected in the circumstances.

"Glad to be with you, m'boy," came the answer. The old man stood, leaning heavily on an ebony cane, at the bottom of the steps. He was gathering his breath in such a laboured way that it might be supposed he had walked, or even run, all the way from Bath.

"I trust you have had a comfortable journey."

The old man laughed testily. "It's never that.

Can't abide travelling, as you know, and my health is never very certain these days."

"Then we are doubly honoured to have you here at this time."

Percival Courtney-Smythe laughed again as he looked at his great nephew. "Couldn't miss your birthday celebration, m'boy. Had to bring the present m'self, you know."

He straightened up a little and started up the steps. His squat frame laboured under the effort. "Mustn't keep your mother waiting out here any longer. Treacherous time of the year."

The earl hurried after him, taking his arm to help him on his way. The countess's pinched features broke into a strained smile at the approach of her relative.

"Uncle Percival! How splendid it is to see you!" She grasped his gloved hands in hers. "Your favourite room overlooking the park is ready, and just how you like it. The carpenter has been in to ensure there can be no draughts from the windows or doors. You have only to speak if you need anything, but I am sure I have forgotten nothing. The fire was lit first thing this morning and I personally made sure that the sheets were well-aired before they were put on the bed."

"Thank you, m'dear." He glanced at Dareth. "I can always be sure of my welcome here. That is one thing I must admit. Always a cordial welcome at Glenbrooke Abbey, even for a worthless creature such as myself."

He gave a gruff laugh which ended in a violent fit of coughing. The countess shot a vexed look at her son but only received a glance of amusement in return.

She transferred her attention back to her guest and said sweetly, "Come inside, Uncle Percival. You will take a chill standing out here so long."

In the hall Latimer relieved the newcomer of his hat, gloves and coat, all of them of an extremely old-fashioned cut.

"Must say you're as handsome as ever, Adeline," he said, as the butler withdrew.

The countess simpered. "And you are the same old flatterer."

He drew a hand across his wig. "I only speak the truth, Adeline. You look not a year older than the day Henry married you."

She looked to her son. "Oh, isn't he kind to say so, Dareth?"

"As Great Uncle Percival said, it's no more than the truth."

The old man pulled at his waistcoat, which was straining at its buttons over his huge corpulence. "If you'll be good enough to have that butler of yours show me to my rooms, I'll change for dinner in a trice and not keep you good people waiting for your victuals any longer."

The countess slipped her arm into his and began to lead him towards the stairs. "You'll not rush for anyone, Uncle Percival. Neither of us is changed yet, as you must have noticed, and there is still ample time for us to rest a while in the drawing room before we retire to change. We tend to keep town hours even when we are rusticating. Habit is hard to change.

"I've already instructed Latimer to delay dinner by an hour, so you have no need to fret. It's been quite a hectic day here, you know. Dareth has been terribly busy with estate business."

She flashed a smile at her son who was following them up the stairs. His returning smile was a wry one. It would be no great surprise to him if his mother charmed his great uncle out of the money—wife or no wife.

"Agents and stewards are all very well," she was saying, "but an estate such as ours needs a heavy hand, and always has done. Diligence is the reason the Glenbrooke estate has always prospered, and," she added, "the reason it always will."

The old man glanced behind him, glad of the chance to pause in his ascent of the great stairway. "Glad to hear you're settling down to it so well, m'boy. I have to admit I doubted that you would. Yes, indeed, I did."

Dareth waved his hand in the air with a gay flourish. "It's the simple life for me, Great Uncle Percival."

His great uncle looked extremely gratified, much to Dareth's vexation, so it seemed the sarcasm so evident in his voice was lost on him.

"Did I hear you mention," his mother ventured, "that you had a present for Dareth?"

They had come to the drawing room and the old man gratefully lowered his body into the nearest chair. "I know it's a little early," he wheezed, "but I wanted to come now. Needed the change. Been recuperating. A chill, you know. Devilish tricky at my time of life."

"Oh, indeed." The countess pulled her shawl about her and looked at him. Her words were loaded with sympathy but her eyes were alight with speculation. Her son placed himself by the window and, glancing at his watch, promised himself no more than five minutes before retiring to his rooms.

Percy Courtney-Smythe looked at the young man. "Came by a silver hunting cup a time back. It dates from the reign of George the First. Thought of you immediately I clapped eyes on it. It will make a pretty display on your desk."

Dareth allowed himself a glance at his mother and saw the light die from her eyes and her countenance take on an expression of horror and dismay.

Managing to keep his own face quite serious, although mirth was making him quake inwardly, he answered, "That is extremely kind of you, sir. I appreciate the thought."

Rousing herself, his mother hurried forward, snatching up a cushion from the sofa. "Here, Uncle Percival," she said quickly, "put this against your back. You must be bruised in every part after your journey. Are you sure you would not prefer this chair by the fire instead?"

"No, no, m'dear," he answered mildly, "I'm quite comfortable where I am."

"Some light refreshment, perhaps?"

"I shall wait for dinner. It is always excellent. But," he added, "perhaps there is still some of that claret I enjoyed so much last time I visited."

"Ah, yes," the countess answered delightedly, "we have kept some especially for you, Uncle Percival." She looked at her son who was standing, arms folded, leaning against the window ledge. "Did I not say, on the last occasion it was brought up, we must keep some for dear Uncle Percival? He enjoys it so much."

Her son's face remained inscrutable. "You did indeed Mama."

She knew him well enough to recognise the mocking look in his eyes and in his words and, hiding her own smile, said quickly, "Do bring that footstool over here, dearest, so that Uncle Percival can rest his legs."

Like a dutiful son and great nephew, the earl did as he was bade, and as the countess arranged a Chinese screen to blot out any draught the old man said, "You will quite spoil me, Adeline."

She laughed gaily. "That is my intention."

Percival Courtney-Smythe sank back into the cushions with a contented smile. "I may never return to Bath."

The earl, unable to contain his amusement a moment longer as his mother fussed around their visitor, turned, apparently to look out of the window.

"You will be welcome to stay for as long as you wish, dear," replied the countess, but her son recognised a certain amount of tension in her voice.

"Being fussed by a beautiful woman is all any man could desire. I should have married, of course, and had a dozen daughters to care for me in my old age. Too late for that now," he added in a slightly more melancholy tone. "But that's why I wished to see you settled in matrimony, Dareth."

The earl turned round again. His demeanour was once more thoughtful. He shot a warning glance at his mother who looked reproachful, and said, "Did you indeed, sir? Your concern is touching."

"Wanted to see m'great, great nephew before I died."

"You may still do so," the countess said eagerly.

The old man shook his head. "No. I'm an old man. I've not long left on this earth, and it's not likely your daughter and that spineless husband of hers will produce anything."

"Oh, really," protested the countess, "that isn't so."

He looked at her without a flicker of interest. "Is she in the family way then?"

The countess blushed and the earl grinned to see her discomfiture. "Not as far as I am aware, but," she hastened to add, "you must remember that they've not been married much above twelve months."

Percival Courtney-Smythe waved a pudgy hand in the air. "If she has a string of brats they won't be Farringdons, will they?"

The countess bit her lip. She longed to tell him, in no uncertain terms, that he wasn't a Farringdon either. His only link was by marriage. In fact he hadn't a drop of aristocratic blood in his veins, but she contented herself by flashing a venomous look towards his back.

"Well," said the old man, addressing himself to the earl, "you may think yourself charitable, m'boy, for the children of the Herndale Foundling Hospital will thank you for it. The bequest will be made in your name, not mine."

"How nice," commented the countess, smiling sourly.

Uncle Percival looked at her. "Thought you'd think so, Adeline. By the by, how is Melissa? Should've asked before."

"Wonderful, just wonderful." The countess flashed an apologetic smile across at her son. "In fact she will be coming here some time this week."

"Good lord!" exclaimed the earl, turning away again, adding beneath his breath, "This is outside of enough."

The countess laughed in an overbright way. "In all the excitement of the past few days, I completely forgot to mention it! How silly of me! Melissa was quite determined to take the opportunity of seeing Uncle Percival whilst he is here."

Percival Courtney-Smythe's eyes narrowed a fraction as he gazed at his great nephew's back. "I seem to recall you never got on well with your sister, Dareth." He laughed. "You used to fight like a pair of prize cocks!"

The countess winced at such vulgarity but forced a smile on to her face. "That was when they were children. They get on perfectly well now. Of course, there is a full ten years' difference in their ages and Dareth and Melissa have widely differing natures."

"Yes, indeed," the old man mused. "Dareth is very much like his father and Melissa, I recall, favours you, Adeline." He then addressed Dareth's back and chuckled, "Excitable woman, your mother."

The earl turned round again and fixed his mother with a steely stare which she was unable to hold. "Yes, I know. She's irresponsible and impulsive too."

The old man then looked uncomfortable. "That's too harsh a judgement, I'm sure."

"I assure you it is not." He started across the room. "I think it is time I changed out of these clothes. . . ."

Just as he reached the door there came a knock and it was opened.

"Dr Bishop is here, my lady. He wishes to see the

countess again. Do you wish to accompany him now or shall I ask him to return later?"

The butler paused, the earl drew in a sharp breath and the countess's eyes grew wide in alarm. For once she was without speech. Their guest heaved his bulk out of the chair and swayed unsteadily on his feet.

"What's this? Are you ill, Adeline?"

The earl stared vexedly at his mother. "I really believe she is," he murmured.

"Why on earth didn't you write and say so? I wouldn't have imposed myself on you at this time."

He looked at his great nephew and if he noticed the flush that had crept up his cheeks he made no mention of it. "It's just as well finances will keep you tied to the estate in future, m'boy. Your mother needs you around. I thought she looked a trifle peaked only didn't like to say so. Yes, I think it is just as well you won't go gallivanting about."

He laughed gruffly and the countess, whose hands had been clasped together in anguish, folded them demurely in front of her. Ignoring the warning look in her son's eye, she drew herself up to full height, which was never considerable, and looked squarely at the old man. "If Dareth has to remain at Glenbrooke Abbey it will not be on *my* account, but because of his wife."

The earl flung the door full open, much to the dismay of Latimer who was waiting his mistress's pleasure. As he strode furiously down the corridor leading to the long gallery he was aware of the startled silence that had followed his mother's declaration.

Then he heard his great uncle say, for the old man's voice was never soft, "Wife! D'you mean to tell me the cub's got riveted after all?"

"I really could strangle you, Mother. I can't think of one good reason why I shouldn't."

The countess, wrapped in a pale pink negligee, lay immobile on a chaise longue in her boudoir while her son paced the room like a restless cat. He was so angry his face was white, making his eyes seem darker by comparison and therefore much angrier.

The countess held a damp handkerchief to her lips. "I wish you would. I cannot conceive why you did not denounce me there and then."

The earl stopped his pacing momentarily. "If I had spoken at that moment I might have choked on my own words."

"You ate practically no dinner."

"For the same reason. All those questions about my 'wife.' What was her background and how did we meet. "They met on the Heath,'" he mocked. "'Fell in love within an hour. Married within a week. Secret weddings are all the rage, you know.'"

"So they are," his mother answered in an aggrieved tone. "I can name three in this past year alone."

"You have the most fertile brain, Mother! Never let it be said otherwise. If only you would set it to work constructively, there would be no end to the wonders you could perform.

"Thank heavens Great Uncle Percival was tired after his journey. I couldn't have borne another second of it."

"I have apologised," she sobbed. "Tell me what more I must do."

"Explain to my great uncle for a start, and then you may explain to Miss Kendricks."

"Oh, I cannot."

He stopped his pacing again. "And if that isn't outside of enough, Melissa is due to arrive within a few days. Are we expected to tell *her* I am married? Great Uncle Percival may have lived in Bath for thirty years but Melissa hasn't, and she isn't likely to swallow your Banbury tales."

"She will think it terribly romantic."

"Melissa may be at times as addle-brained as you, Mother, but her husband certainly is not."

She struggled to a sitting position. "I don't have to endure this sauce from you, Dareth. I am after all your mother. . . ."

"Heaven help me for it."

". . . and entitled to some respect." She drew the negligee tighter around her. "I want nothing for myself, as you well know." Her face crumpled. "I couldn't bear to hear him gloat so."

The anger drained out of the earl at seeing such a woebegone expression on the face of his mother. He crossed the room, sat down at the end of the chaise longue and took her hand in his. "Surely you know," he said gently, "such a ruse could not possibly succeed."

"Yes, I do see it now. What is to be done? I shall never be able to hold up my head to my own servants, let alone my own family. Even Fraser is quite taken with her. How is it all to be set to rights?" And then, irrelevantly, "Oh, I do wish you would drive with more care."

His eyes widened momentarily. "It is generally agreed that I am an excellent whip. If you are determined to shift the blame elsewhere you may place it on the driver of the postchaise which almost pushed me into the ditch."

Just at that moment Fraser came in and dropped a deep curtsey. "Will there be anything else you'll be wanting tonight, my lady?"

The countess waved a hand at her in an almost preoccupied way. "No, you may retire now if you wish, Fraser."

The woman nodded stiffly and then, giving the earl a pointedly icy look, she said, "I think I'll go and sit with the invalid for a while."

"As you wish," answered her mistress, waving her hand again.

When the woman had gone, the earl looked at his mother in some amusement. "I fear I have offended the good Fraser in some way, although I cannot recall how. Her manner towards me was decidedly chilly just now."

A more normal twinkle returned to the countess's eye. "My dearest, is it not obvious?" When he still remained so obviously mystified she went on, "You have not visited Miss Kendricks since your arrival, and seeing the servants believe her to be your wife, you may be considered neglectful."

"Good grief! You do not expect me to dance attendance on her."

His mother sighed. "No, dear."

"Supposing," he said thoughtfully, "Great Uncle Percival was taken in by this charade, if I were to go along with it—which I am not!" he added quickly as the light kindled in his mother's eyes again. "What would we do with Miss Kendricks afterwards? You have not considered that, I'll wager."

The countess swung her satin-slippered feet to the floor. "There you are wrong. I would, as I have already intimated, find her an exceptional position."

"I doubt if Great Uncle Percival will be so obliging as to die immediately on his return to Bath," said the earl drily. "He will surely want news of her in the future, and not that she is in service in some middle-class household."

"You could always find marriage abominable and part," she said thoughtfully. "It is not entirely unknown for such hasty marriages to fail before long." Then brightening considerably went on, "It would be no less than the truth. Uncle Percival could then, if he so wished, cut you out of his will and you could repay the wedding gift. . . ."

"Such unneccessary complications, Mother."

She grasped his hand eagerly. "If only you would go along with this for now, dearest. I would never ask another favour of you as long as I live." At this her son's eyebrows rose a fraction. "I no longer care a fig for his fortune, but I live in dread of appearing a fool. He has always thought me a goose, you know. He may take Miss Kendricks in dislike and leave his money to the hospital anyway. I don't care as long as he does not see me as a fool, Dareth, and the servants do not know what a goose I've been. I couldn't bear that. Uncle Percival would gloat so. Oh, please, I beg of you, don't do that to me. I couldn't bear it."

Her eyes were full of appeal. "If your conscience troubles you, Dareth, you may give away the money, or refuse it, as you will. The matter of the will is of the least importance to me now. I know I don't deserve your charity. . . ."

Her eyes filled with tears and she was unable to continue. Her son withdrew his hand and got to his feet. He towered over her. Fingering his quizzing glass he gazed at her thoughtfully for a moment or two.

"I would not want you to appear a fool, Mother," he said, breaking, a seemingly interminable silence. "You know I wouldn't deliberately inflict that upon you. Foolish as you are, you mean no harm."

"Oh, Dareth, my love."

"And I admit for the moment I see no way out of this business."

"I am so grateful!" she said, clasping her hands together.

"Don't be grateful. Just heed your tongue in future. I don't ever want to have such a problem again."

"I will be careful, Dareth. Oh, certainly I will. You need have no fear of that."

The earl turned away. How often in the past he had heard her utter this same promise to his late father, yet like his father he could not maintain an anger towards her for long. The trouble always was her inability to see the harm in any of her schemes; she could only see the good.

"As Miss Kendricks already believes she is the Countess of Glenbrooke she may as well continue to think so for a few more days. The harm of discovering she is not will be no greater for waiting. She may be stronger by the time our visitors depart."

"Precisely my thoughts," his mother said eagerly.

"Afterwards we shall ensure that Miss Kendricks is well taken care of. She will find this matter, ultimately, has been to her advantage."

"Naturally. You can depend on it, Dareth."

When he said nothing more she jumped up and

threw her arms around his neck. "I don't deserve your goodness."

He laughed then at the passion in her declaration and disentangled himself from her embrace. "No, you certainly do not. And I do not deserve the damage you are doing to my neckcloth."

She drew away and smiled at him tremulously. "It is very well tied tonight, Dareth. Did you spoil many before you achieved such perfection?"

"No more than a half dozen," he answered with no particular interest. "Do you realise," he said a moment later, "that this, in effect, makes you the Dowager Countess. . . ?"

The countess clapped one hand to her lips. "Oh, heavens, so it does. How grim."

"It serves you right. I may even make this an excuse to have your belongings removed to the Dower House."

Her eyes grew large. "You would not!"

He smiled then. "Grandmama lived there quite happily for many years, I recall."

The countess grimaced. "I am quite unlike your grandmama."

"It would be far less than you deserve."

"I shall never cause you any more trouble, I promise."

"We shall see," he answered with a heartfelt sigh.

He moved towards the door and she said, frowning slightly, "You *will* go along with this until Uncle Percival has gone?"

"Certainly, up to a point. Great Uncle Percival will be glad to see me working very hard on the estate during his stay. I may even don a smock and work out in the fields." His ironic smile faded. "Anything to keep me out of the way of this little intrigue."

She took one step forward. "But you will visit Miss Kendricks."

"Certainly not! It is enough that for the moment she bears my name. What would I possibly say to her?"

"If you don't, it will look so odd, Dareth."

"It will have to look odd, Mother, I'm afraid, or," he added, reaching for the door knob, "perhaps you would prefer me to share her bedchamber too?"

"Don't be vulgar, Dareth," retorted the countess.

His eyebrows rose a fraction. "If I don't," he mocked, "it will look so odd."

The countess relaxed. "You are only funning. You have a cruel sense of humour when you so choose. It's as well I know you."

"Funning?" he asked with a great air of surprise. "I just thought I could derive some amusement from the situation."

"You could easily take advantage of her; she believes you to be her husband," said the countess in sudden realisation.

"Exactly."

The countess bridled. "She is a dear, sweet, innocent child, Dareth. Let me tell you she is not at all like the females you are used to."

"All the better," he insisted. "A dear, sweet, innocent child is quite the thing to tempt a jaded palate such as mine." At the sight of her dismay his smile faded and he said briskly, "Have no fear for her innocence, Mother. She is most certainly not to my taste, jaded palate or no. You are quite correct in that assumption. You cannot *always* be wrong.

"I shall go along with this charade in as much as not telling Great Uncle Percival of your foolishness. What I will not do is contribute to the deception by any concrete act or word."

"I cannot understand your scruples," his mother declared. "You must have been involved in far worse larks than this."

He came back to her then and kissed her lightly on the cheek. "But nothing quite so dishonourable as this, Mama."

She relaxed again at the fondness in his voice and as he went back to the door she ventured hopefully, "You *will* go to see her, Dareth?"

"Definitely not."

Chapter Five

Lucinda gazed around her, at the vast infinity of the room in which she had been placed. This morning the heavy velvet curtains had been drawn back from the windows and the sunshine flowed in unrestrained. It was a good omen, yet Lucinda was not cheered by it.

She still felt dazed. Her head had almost burst the previous evening with the effort of trying to remember anything at all, but it was to no avail. She had been told she was the Countess of Glenbrooke, and although she had no idea herself of her identity she had at first refused to believe it. It seemed, somehow, quite unlikely although to refute it would put her sanity in doubt. The accident, it would appear, had done more than take away her memory; it had upset the balance of her emotions.

Her own name was Lucinda and her husband's was Dareth, she had been told, and although she repeated both names time and time again, they refused to become familiar to her.

Surely something must seem familiar, she reasoned. Something must strike a chord in her memory before long. It was unfortunate that this was her first visit to Glenbrooke Abbey so she could not even expect anyone or anything to appear familiar to her here. Only her husband. . . .

She fingered the lace at the edge of her sleeve. The bedgown was of the finest satin and lace, delightfully frothy and feminine, and even that seemed strange.

She sank back into the pillows. It was no use teasing her brain any more. She just could not remember anything beyond the moment she awoke in this bed yesterday afternoon. The doctor said she had nothing to worry about; her memory would return as she gradually recovered from the shock of the accident, but he hadn't spoken convincingly. And no one had explained in great detail what exactly had happened to cause her so grievous an injury. The countess, when questioned, always spoke of it vaguely.

It was hard for Lucinda to credit that she was a new bride. She felt almost hysterical at the thought of being married to a man she couldn't recall. She was quite horrified to discover that she didn't know whether her husband was short and fat or tall and thin, good humoured or disagreeable, handsome or plain. What is more, she didn't *feel* married.

Fraser had laughed when she had voiced this sentiment, saying, "You haven't been wed long enough yet!"

At least her mother-in-law was not at all alarming. Adeline was the most beautiful woman she had ever seen, although, of course, she couldn't recall ever seeing anyone else. And Lucinda thought she looked far too young to have grownup children. The countess was so very sympathetic too. She seemed to understand how horrific it was to wake up and find everything and everyone strange, as if she had been born just at that moment.

As Lucinda lay, deep in contemplation, Fraser came up to the bed and smiled fondly down at the girl of whom she had taken charge. Having known the earl since the day he was born, and his mother a good deal longer, and being aware of the many scrapes out of which his father had had to extricate him, privately Fraser was surprised that he had brought such a sweet girl home as his bride. Which went to prove, as she had told Adams, the under-butler, only that morning, one should never judge harshly.

"Shall I read you a little from this volume of Keats? Her ladyship loves it. Or perhaps you don't like Keats? He's not to everyone's taste, and I must admit I don't understand a word of it myself."

Lucinda looked up at her as she settled her ample form into a chair by the bed. "I don't know what I like or what I don't like, Fraser. And shouldn't you be attending the countess instead of being here with me?"

Fraser smiled. "Her ladyship has been kind enough to release me to attend you while you need me. Not that there's been a great deal for me to do of late, you understand. Not since the countess was widowed and has been in mourning this past twelve-month. It was different when his lordship—the sixth earl—was alive. There was enough for me to do then, I can tell you."

Avid for as much information as she could get, Lucinda listened in fascination. "Do tell me more," she begged.

Eager to oblige the woman licked her lips. "There were constant balls, routs, card parties and breakfasts at Grosvenor Square." Fraser's rosy-apple face beamed at the recollection. "Those were marvellous times, and her ladyship had to be dressed accordingly and in the very latest style, mind you. Everyone looked to the countess to see what was the latest style. Why, I recall when it took hours, simply hours, to dress and powder her hair. And her ladyship was one of the first ladies in London to wear a muslin dress in the classic style. It was almost transparent and that caused a ruction in certain circles."

Fraser chuckled and Lucinda laughed. "She sounds marvellous."

"She's outrageous at times, but good natured in spite of it. Wouldn't do a fly a mite of harm, wouldn't my lady. But she's been in some scrapes. Some of them only I know about. There's been times when she's been a quake for fear the earl would find out, though he was never cross with her for long, whatever she did. Ah, he was a lovely man. Knew every member of the staff by name, even the kitchen maids, and made it his business to ask after them."

"How did he die? Was it very sudden?"

Fraser looked suddenly grim. "Aye, that it was. Just after the lady Melissa was married. The family came back to the country and brought a crowd with them. One night the gentlemen stayed down even later than usual, gambling and drinking. It was the usual type of house party. The earl and countess were great ones for entertaining.

"The earl was the last one down that night. I'll remember it until the the day I die. Raving drunk he was, it's said. When his man came down to put him to bed—something he'd done a time or two—he couldn't find him. He wasn't in the card room or anywhere else in the house. All the servants were called out of their beds to help search. They didn't find him until dawn—drowned in the trout stream."

Lucinda gasped. "How terrible."

"Aye, terrible enough for her ladyship," answered Fraser sadly. "They were a rarely devoted pair, for all his hell-raising ways. My poor countess cried every night for months, and there's only me who knows about it. She laughs that readily no one would ever believe it of her."

"It must have been a dreadful time for her," said Lucinda sympathetically. "Did anyone know what had happened?"

Fraser shrugged slightly. "Possibly he wanted some air, to sober himself up, but being so deep in his cups the poor man didn't know what he was doing.

"His son was the last to go up that night. He'd left his father in a stupor. He went upstairs and told his man to go and fetch him to bed, but by the time Grayson went down his lordship had gone."

Lucinda listened wide-eyed as Fraser related the tale of tragedy. "Of course," the woman went on, warming to the story, "there were some who were quick to say the seventh earl did it." It was many a day since she'd had such a willing listener.

"Dareth," gasped Lucinda, flushing immediately at the use of so unfamiliar a name.

Fraser's eyes shifted away. "Beggin' your pardon, my lady. I was forgetting myself."

Lucinda sat up in the bed. "Do you mean to tell me people actually suspected my husband of making away with his own father?"

"Now, now," said Fraser, hastily getting to her feet, "let's have none of this excitement or Dr. Bishop'll have my head on a platter. My tongue's always been too nimble. I should've kept my lip buttoned."

"But is it true?"

"No, of course it isn't. I've known the earl since the day he was born to my lady, and for all the hellrake ways he inherited from his father and his grandfather before him, he'd not do anyone a mite of harm, much less his father, who he idolised."

At such an impassioned defence of the man she had married, Lucinda relaxed a little.

Fraser sighed. "I'm only repeating a story. There's always plenty of those when someone has a position of importance. You'll hear it soon enough when you're out and about. There are many who are jealous of the present earl and of his father before him. And what with the first earl being such a rum creature, such gossip was to be expected, especially as his lordship was the last one to see his father alive. You should hear some of the things they've said about the countess, and none of those tales had a penn'orth of truth in them."

Lucinda sank back into the pillows. "How horrible some people can be. I can hardly credit it."

Fraser chuckled. "You'll get used to the ways of Society if you're not used to them already," she said, adding wryly, "seeing as you're the new countess, you'll have to."

Lucinda stared unseeingly ahead. Fraser's words had troubled her. Could there be any truth in the story? Surely not, Lucinda was sure she would have married only for love, and she certainly could never love any man remotely capable of such a dastardly crime. The trouble was, she didn't know....

She began to pluck at the covers as Fraser said, "You're a better colour today, my lady. Dr Bishop said you can get up for a while this afternoon."

"I shall be glad to do so," the girl replied without much enthusiasm. "I only wish my trunk had arrived."

"I just don't know what could have become of it, but never fret: her ladyship has brought out some of Lady Melissa's gowns and I've pressed them for you. Perhaps they're not as good or as fashionable as my lady's own gowns but they'll fit all right. Fraser'll see to that."

Lucinda rallied a little. "You are both too good." She put one hand to her head. "That dreadful pain has gone, but I still remember nothing. It's so tiresome. I try so hard, but my mind's a total blank."

"Now, you mustn't tease yourself, my lady. You don't want to bring on a brain fever. It'll all come back in time if you let things be."

"I want to remember *now*," said Lucinda despairingly. "I feel it's important that I do so."

"It's not as important as getting you better."

The woman walked away from the bed. "Fraser," said Lucinda, and when the woman came back she looked away, plucking at the sheet again. "Why has my husband not called in to see me?"

The expression on the servant's face became a little strained. "All sorts of reasons, my lady. He's not been home for months and there's a great deal for him to do on the estate. Her ladyship was only saying so this very morning. And of course Mr Courtney-Smythe arrived from Bath yesterday. He's a demanding old codger and no mistake. He keeps everyone on their toes, dancing attendance. And of course you have been insensible for a lot of the time you've been here. Men don't like to be in the presence of illness. He'll be along all in good time, don't you fret."

The woebegone expression remained on Lucinda's face. "You can't imagine how tiresome it is not to be able to remember one's own husband. I have no idea what he looks like!"

Fraser fumbled in the pocket of her apron. "I was forgetting. I've got something for you to see. I've borrowed this from her ladyship's room. Thought you'd like to see it."

It was a miniature. Lucinda took it rather reluctantly, dreading now to look upon the face of the man she had married. Slowly she dropped her eyes to gaze upon the earl's likeness. It was a relief to discover that his countenance was a handsome one although his expression was a mite severe. But she told herself comfortingly, such studies usually did show a more sober disposition. As she gazed at the miniature, deriving some comfort from it, she still felt nothing but apprehension.

Fraser watched her eagerly. "It was done five years ago but it's a good likeness. Does it mean anything to you?"

Lucinda's fingers were shaking when she finally handed it back. She nodded her head. "I'm sure," she said, swallowing noisily, "I have seen him before. He doesn't look altogether strange to me."

"Nor so alarming," added Fraser, smiling wryly. "Did you think you might be married to a monstrous old man?"

"Not that. Not after seeing his mother. But I was a little afraid, I admit. Who wouldn't be?"

"Well, let me tell you something, my lady; when you take up residence in Grosvenor Square—and there's not a finer mansion in the whole city—and you start your entertaining as the new countess of Glenbrooke, there'll not be a maiden in the whole of society who won't envy you."

Lucinda answered with a weak smile. Entertaining the ton. Lucinda could not imagine herself capable.

After a moment's consideration of Lucinda's pale face, the servant suggested, "Shall I make you one of my tisanes, my lady? It will make you feel better, I'm sure. Her ladyship vouches by them. They've revived her on many an occasion."

"I should like that, Fraser. Her ladyship cannot be wrong."

Fraser bobbed a curtsey. "I'll not be longer than a few minutes, my lady. Try to doze while I'm gone. You'll feel a mite better for it."

Lucinda nodded. Her head was beginning to ache from the effort of talking and listening. She would be glad of being on her own for a while, to search her mind again for any hopeful glimmer of remembrance; to discover that she was the kind of wife worthy of the Earl of Glenbrooke.

But it was not to be. No sooner had she closed her eyes than she heard Fraser talking to someone at the door. At first she thought it must be Dr Bishop come to see her, full of his mirthless smiles and emptily reassuring words. And then she realised that the man's voice was nothing like that of the physician's.

She sat up sharply in the bed, pulling back the curtains, but she could see only Fraser from where she lay. Lucinda automatically smoothed her hair and pulled the sheets up higher.

Then the door closed as he came into the room. As Fraser had said, he did not look so alarming but he was older than she had expected, again because the countess looked so very young. Tears pricked at her eyes; he might well have been a total stranger for the memory he stirred in her.

It was, however, some relief for her to see that he too was feeling awkward and embarrassed, even though she sensed it was wholly out of character. He had entered the room as if some unseen hand was pushing him forward.

She smiled shyly as he approached; he seemed to have taken an age to cross the room. Fingering a gold seal that dangled from his waistcoat he said, "I hope you are feeling better."

There was a vexed frown marring his otherwise

handsome features as he addressed her. To Lucinda's dismay it appeared that he was actually hostile. How tiresome he must find me, she thought, and so I am. She could not blame him his irritation, but she longed to hear him utter a reassuring word.

She stared down at the counterpane which was embroidered with the lion, the lamb, the myrtle and the rose which made up the Glenbrooke crest. "Very much better, my lord," she managed to say.

For a moment as he looked around he seemed ready to excuse himself, then he drew a chair close to the bed and eased himself into it. Lucinda, in her confusion, did not know whether she was glad or not.

"I hope you are comfortable here."

"Oh very," she answered with a little more enthusiasm. "Your mother and Fraser have been exceedingly kind, and everything possible has been done for my comfort."

At this prim little speech he smiled but it was a strained smile. "And your head? I am persuaded it must be very sore."

She looked at him then, quickly and then away again. "The pain has gone."

He looked at her anxiously. "Can you yet remember?"

She shook her head and he seemed to relax into the chair. In truth he was vexed. What had originated as a kindly deed, when he had brought her to the house for aid, had developed into the most tiresome of burdens.

Short of refuting publicly the story of his marriage—and he had yet to discover an honourable
way of doing so—he had been determined to have
no more to do with the matter. But, naturally, it
was not, as the earl was discovering, so easy to remain aloof especially when his mother was determined that he should not do so.

Despite his flat refusal the previous evening to
visit the girl, his mother had, most unfairly he
reckoned, pressed him again this morning; this
time in the presence of Great Uncle Percival and
to refuse would have looked exceedingly odd.
Were it not for the infamous pretence forced
upon him by his impulsive mama, the earl might
have been willing to pay his respects to the invalid. But he had, on this occasion, been forced to
agree to his mother's suggestion. And seeing the
approving smile on his great uncle's face did nothing to improve the earl's humour. He had come to
the King's Bedchamber with the greatest reluctance, assuming that it would be a quick visit
with the formidable Fraser, who had always
alarmed him as a child, in attendance. Now, to
add to his annoyance, his mother's personal servant
had excused herself, and with a great deal of
uncharacteristic coyness about her demeanor she
had left the two for, apparently, an intimate coze,
which did not suit the earl's already wounded
sense of propriety one bit.

As it was, he could hardly bear to look upon the
girl. His pride was outraged at the very idea that

his family and servants would believe him wed to this slip of a girl with nothing in the world to recommend her but a pair of exceedingly appealing green eyes.

He drew out his watch and glanced at it as the sudden and lengthy silence began to weigh upon them both. As he slipped it back into the pocket of his waistcoat Lucinda said quickly, "You must be, I'm persuaded, very busy. It was kind of you to spare the time to call in on me, but pray don't allow me to detain you further."

The earl was startled at her perceptiveness of his anxiety to be away. He had not thought it so obvious, although on second thoughts he realised he had done little to hide it.

All at once, seeing the fear and bewilderment in the girl's eyes he was remorseful and smiled quite kindly at her. After all, he reasoned, Lucinda Kendricks was quite innocent and not deserving of his anger, especially as he could imagine some of the tortured thoughts running through her mind at that very moment.

"I have," he admitted, in a gentle tone, "much to do after so long an absence. I do have an appointment with my steward this morning, but that would not," he went on, swallowing slightly, "prevent me from visiting you first."

"You are too kind," she murmured, lowering her eyes again.

After eyeing the forlorn figure for a moment or

two he said, rather impulsively, "You have, I think, grown a great deal thinner."

She looked at him appealingly. "Have I? I cannot recall."

He smiled again. "Don't let it tease you. You will soon be recovered completely. I am convinced of it."

At such kind words her reserve crumbled. Impulsively she leaned over and grasped his hand tightly. The heavy seal ring he wore on his little finger cut into her flesh, but she was hardly aware of it.

"Oh, Dareth, I'm sorry I'm such a tiresome burden on you!"

His eyes opened wide in alarm at such an impassioned plea. Her innocent use of his name affected him profoundly, although in what way he was hard put to name. His flesh seemed to burn beneath hers and as he got to his feet he extricated himself from her importuning hand.

"Please don't consider yourself that, my dear," he said quickly. "It will all come right in the end, you'll see," he added, unconsciously echoing his mother's words.

So saying, he bowed slightly to her and without waiting a moment longer he hurried towards the door, aware that she was following him with a pair of eyes wide with fear. Lucinda sank back into the pillows again, not in the least comforted by his last clumsy attempt to reassure her. There was nothing of the affectionate husband in his manner, and she didn't wonder. She must have been, before the accident, quite a different woman to have attracted such a handsome and personable man as a husband. No doubt he was finding her as strange as she was finding him.

During the past twenty-four hours she had been determined not to break down, but as the door closed behind him the tears began to prick at her eyes again and before she could stop them they were coursing down her cheeks in a never-ending stream.

By the time he had reached the end of the long gallery, the earl's anger had abated considerably, but he vowed to occupy himself fully in the future and never again be subjected to such an embarrassing interview.

However, when he reached the top of the stairs an excited scene in the hall below met his eyes. His mother and sister were embracing excitedly whilst his brother-in-law and another man were standing nearby being divested of their outdoor clothes.

Melissa's brown curls bobbed up and down in excitement as the earl heard her utter, "Married, Mama! Dareth? Oh, how splendid! And isn't it just like him to escape all the fuss?"

On seeing both his sister's excitement and such a preponderance of new visitors, he was very much tempted to turn and slip out of the house by way of the back stairs. But not possessing a cowardly nature, and never before turning his back on difficulties, he took a deep breath and started down the stairs. His sister saw him immediately and hurried to greet him. He enveloped her in his arms and they embraced for a moment or two before she drew away, her eyes agleam with pleasure.

"Dareth, this is the most wonderful news I could ever wish to hear."

On hearing such a statement so genuinely spoken, the earl was once more displeased. His sister regarded him carefully. "I do declare you look better for it already. Does he not, Hugo?"

He met his mother's eye and she cast him an apologetic look, and it was obvious she was feeling numerous qualms as the matter, with the introduction of more visitors, became even more complex.

The earl's brother-in-law came forward then and proferred his hand. He was a tall, thin man, no taller than the earl but seeming so because of his leaness. And he was dressed in an extremly foppish style which offended the earl's excellent sense of dress. The points of his shirt collar were so high and so stiff that the man could hardly move his head. His waistcoat, so richly adorned with various chains, fobs and seals, was of a bright red and mauve pattern, and his coat was festooned with mother-of-pearl buttons so big that they could be used instead as saucers.

It was obvious the fellow thought himself the very tulip of fashion, but not possessing the caustic tongue of his friend, Beau Brummell, the earl did not see fit to shatter his brother-in-law's illusion on that point.

However, as the earl took his brother-in-law's hand the man said, in a decidedly affected air, which never failed to irritate him, "Good for you, Glenbrooke. Felicitations are in order. Allow me to congratulate you."

The earl murmured his thanks and, catching the eye of the other man, nodded briefly to him. Because of his sister, Dareth was willing to tolerate her husband, Hugo, but he was incensed at the idea of also—in addition to all his present tribulations—having to tolerate Sir Hugo's brother, Digby, who was an even less endearing character, and had even less of a sense of style to recommend him.

"Accept my congratulations too, Glenbrooke," said Digby, limping forward to join the family group.

The earl accepted the man's good wishes with an abrupt inclination of his head.

"I do hope you don't mind Digby coming too," Melissa said, wide-eyed, looking from her brother to the countess. "We simply couldn't leave him alone whilst he is still convalescent, and we thought a change of air and new company must be good for him after being laid up for so many months."

"No, no," her mother assured her quickly, flashing a strained smile at the earl who was rapidly wishing himself elsewhere. "Lieutenant Stacey is of course most welcome. Isn't that so, Dareth?"

The earl's smile was a trifle strained but he managed to say in the most urbane manner, "It is quite a pleasure, I admit, to be host to one of the country's heroes. Of course," he added in much the same tone of charm, "I am assuming you received your wound advancing towards the enemy. There are so many ways of receiving shot in the leg. I know of one member of the forces who shot himself while he was cleaning his gun."

Digby Stacey flushed darkly and allowed his quizzing glass, through which he had been peering at the earl, to drop.

Melissa laughed gaily. "How amusing you are, Dareth. Such a droll sense of humour. Oh, I'm in a fever of impatience. When am I to meet your bride?"

"Tomorrow at the earliest, I'm afraid," her mother said quickly. "Lucinda has been a trifle unwell. There was a small accident on the road." Melissa gasped in dismay and her mother went on to assure her, "She will be quite recovered in a day or so, have no fear, but she is not on any account to be bombarded with questions."

"Oh dear," said Melissa, giving her brother a sympathetic glance. "I am indeed sorry to hear of this accident. I can hardly wait to meet her, I confess. A secret wedding is so sublime. I wonder I didn't think of it myself."

She dimpled and glanced at her husband who

smiled back fondly. She slipped her arm into Dareth's. "I do so want to be her friend, dearest. And I'm doubly delighted to hear of your marriage because Hugo and I are so superbly happy. I want you to be so happy too, although I declare no one could equal our happiness."

"Your sentiments, Melissa, are appreciated," answered her brother.

Digby Stacey, having recovered his humour, said languidly, "Have I the honour of already knowing the bride?"

The earl smiled urbanely. "It is most unlikely, Lieutenant Stacey."

"Then, I take it she is not an acquaintance of Miss Kingsley?"

The earl's face darkened. "By no means, Lieutenant Stacey."

As the countess moved forward to avert a clash of personalities, Lieutenant Stacey was not to be done out of his rejoinder. "An acquaintance of Mrs Cartwright perhaps?"

The earl's countenance grew even more stormy and his mother said quickly, "Oh, do let us go upstairs and see Uncle Percival. He has been longing for a sight of you. It must almost be time for luncheon and you people must be famished."

All except the earl allowed themselves to be herded towards the stairs. After taking a few steps Melissa halted and turned to face her mother.

"Mama, all this excitement over Dareth's marriage has put it quite out of my mind!"

"What, dearest?" enquired her mother.

"Hugo and I have something exciting to reveal too. Quite the most wonderful news. I am going to be a mama!"

After a moment's stunned silence the countess clasped her hands together in delight. "That is indeed splendid news. Are you quite well?"

"Perfectly," came the ebullient answer.

"Should you have travelled? I'm persuaded it was most unwise."

Melissa laughed. "Did you allow yourself to be coddled when you were in this condition, Mama?"

The countess smiled wryly. "Of course not." She glanced back at her son and her smile faded a little. Hurriedly she said, "Melissa, dearest, show Hugo and Lieutenant Stacey to the drawing room. Uncle Percival so loves company; he will think we've deserted him. I shall join you in a moment or two."

Melissa's gay chatter could still be heard as she made her way up the great staircase, flanked by an attentive husband and brother-in-law.

The countess crossed the hall swiftly. "Dareth, have you seen Miss Kendricks this morning?" she asked in an unusually hushed voice.

"I had but little choice," he answered, eyeing her severely now that the social niceties need no longer be maintained.

Ignoring the irony in his tone, she said, "And how did you find her?"

"Insipid, and the most unlikely countess I have ever come across. Mrs Cartwright would have done as well. I cannot imagine what possessed me to agree to this farce."

"You agreed because you could think of nothing else to do," answered his mother truthfully.

"And now Digby Stacey is involved too. I'm beginning to doubt my own sanity."

The countess's eyes widened in alarm. "You do not mean to go back on your word?"

"I can hardly do so now, Mother."

"You really are very trying this morning, Dareth."

"Perhaps it is because I have had a very trying morning."

"Do try to bear up, dearest. What was said between you?"

The earl's eyebrows rose a fraction. "Do you wish me to recount all of it? It makes exceedingly dull listening, I assure you."

"Naturally not," she snapped, her patience dwindling rapidly. "Was she at all distressed to see you?"

The earl drew in a sharp breath, recalling those pale, thin hands which clutched tightly at the bedcovers. "Confused, and a little distressed on my behalf, which I found embarrassing. I feel she was desperately trying to recall what she cannot possibly remember."

"Poor child," sighed his mother, and then, more briskly, "It cannot last for long. Melissa and

Hugo are here for only a day or two. They just wish to pay their respects to Uncle Percival."

The earl smiled wryly. "I can imagine why."

His mother stared at him blankly. "And what, may I ask, is that supposed to signify?"

"Only think, Mother, a child on the way. . . ."

The countess smiled. "Isn't that splendid?" Her smile faded. "Good grief! Uncle Percival wouldn't make *it* his beneficiary. He has already said so."

The earl smiled tightly. "That does not mean he cannot change his mind. It would be a considerable relief to me if he did," adding wryly, "if it were not for the possibility of Digby Stacey enjoying the use of it."

He started towards the door and the countess came out of her thoughts into which his last statement had thrust her. "Where are you going?"

"To attend to matters of business." He accepted his hat, gloves and riding whip from the footman in attendance.

"But what of our guests?"

He smiled mischievously. "Yours can be the exclusive and doubtful pleasure of entertaining them. I'm sure you'll find no hardship in answering their questions. It may test your ingenuity somewhat but not unbearably. Miss Kendricks cannot refute anything you say. At least," he added heartlessly, "not yet."

The countess looked vexed. "I shall face up to

that calamity when it occurs, even though I feel that this ruse will be the ruination of me."

"Us," her son amended. "And won't Digby Stacey enjoy *that*. That creature becomes more of a toad with every month that passes."

"I hope you will be civil to Lieutenant Stacey while he is our guest."

"An uninvited guest," he pointed out. "And I always do try to be civil, Mother, only he makes it exceedingly difficult for me to succeed."

As she brushed a minuscule fleck of dust from the shoulder of his jacket, he caught her hand in his and looked down at her laughingly. "Perhaps Lieutenant Stacey's presence will give me some much needed entertainment. I always enjoy my sport with him."

"Dareth," said his mother in a warning tone, and then, realising he was laughing, smiled too.

He regarded her for a moment or two before saying, "In addition to being consigned to the status of dowager this week, you are also about to become a grandmother. How time does fly!"

She gasped. "A grandmother. Oh, heavens, I am not old enough."

"You deserve some punishment for what you have done this week."

She regarded him sombrely then. "If you were indeed married, dearest, it would afford me the greatest delight. As for Melissa, I await my first grandchild with the greatest degree of impatience, even if it does herald the onset of old age." She pressed one hand to her back. "I do believe I feel a twinge of rheumatism already."

He laughed and lifted her hand to his lips. "Dearest, Mama, you will never grow old. But," he added, "for all of us there comes a time when we must grow up!"

She laughed in delight and then, a moment later, said, "Do you intend to return in time to join us for luncheon?"

He let her hand go. "Do not depend on it. In fact, Mother, do not expect to see me very much at all until Great Uncle Percival returns to Bath and we can dispense with all pretence."

The countess looked shocked. "You must attend to Miss Kendricks when she is up, Dareth, and she most certainly will be up tomorrow at the very latest."

"I have no intention in repeating our embarrassing confrontation of this morning." He placed his hat at a jaunty angle and when it was fixed to his satisfaction he went to the door, adding, "And if you persist in engineering one I shall not content myself by being out of the house most of the day, I shall probably join a regiment and go out to the Peninsula to Wellesley's men."

So saying he marched out of the house, leaving his mother staring after him, wide-eyed and incredulous, not knowing whether he was jesting or not.

Chapter Six

"Good grief!" exclaimed the earl the very next afternoon as Lucinda came slowly down the stairs. "Did you say Fraser is a marvel, Mother? I declare she is a witch."

Lucinda flushed under his scrutiny but was nevertheless pleased to see Dareth's obvious admiration. She had not heard his muttered exclamation to his mother but she could see the undisguised admiration in his eyes.

She had been up briefly the previous afternoon and the interview with the earl, which had such an unintentionally disastrous effect upon her, had not hindered the improvement in her health. Dr Bishop, when he called, proclaimed himself pleased with her progress and again reiterated his certainty that her memory would soon return and a degree of patience was all that was required until it did so.

At this pronouncement she had retorted, "I do

indeed hope you may be correct, doctor, for if you are wrong my marriage will collapse. My husband, I fear, is not of a patient nature."

Fraser this morning had put before her a dazzling array of the most beautiful gowns Lucinda was sure she had ever seen. She was hard put to choose between the blue cambric, the yellow muslin, the cream and blue chintz, or the white batiste with pink satin ribbons. The blue cambric was the plainest and for some reason Lucinda chose that one. She could not, somehow, imagine herself in any of the others, magnificent as they were.

She allowed Fraser to fit it on her and make the necessary alterations while she sat by the window wrapped in a heavy velvet negligee that had also once belonged to Lady Melissa Farringdon. When the alterations were done, Lucinda allowed Fraser to button her into the dress.

"All the Lady Melissa's wedding clothes have hook and eye fastenings," said the dresser. "They are much easier to manage. Such a useful invention."

When Fraser had finished her ministrations Lucinda was allowed to look at herself in the chevel mirror and as she caught sight of her reflection she gasped. Not only had the blue cambric gown been made to fit perfectly but her honey-blonde hair had been caught up into a frothy confusion of curls in ribbons that perfectly matched the dress.

"Oh, I look nothing like myself!" she cried, twirling round in delight.

Fraser chuckled. "How would you know, my lady? You can't remember *what* you are like and there's the truth of it." The woman's expression turned to one of satisfaction. "You look a good deal bonnier than you did when I first clapped eyes on you."

Lucinda frowned slightly. "I cannot help but feel I am not used to this kind of life, Fraser. Everything is so strange to me."

Fraser bustled over to the dresser. "Nor you are, my lady. There are few enough establishments as big or as grand as this one. But you've only to look at you to know you're a lady."

"Oh, do you really think so, Fraser?" she asked hopefully. "I do hope you are correct. I cannot help but feel I am not worthy of his lordship. He seems in every way so superior."

Fraser turned to smile fondly at her charge. "'Tis only his manner, my lady. No doubting if you could but recall, you'd remember quite another side to his character."

Lucinda looked unconvinced, but she allowed Fraser to drape a silk shawl about her shoulders. After she had dabbed some rouge onto her pale cheeks, the servant stood back to admire her work.

"Your colour is much better, but a little artificial aid never comes amiss. No doubting a breath of air will bring the roses to your cheeks again."

Lucinda's eyes grew wide. "Fraser, I cannot go out. Everyone is down there!"

"You cannot remain here for ever. Lady Melissa, Sir Hugo and Lieutenant Stacey have gone visiting friends at Staveborough, so there's only the earl and the countess at home, and the earl," at this her facial muscles stiffened slightly, "is usually out on the estate going about his business. You've no cause to be afeared of meeting anyone, my dear. Even Mr Courtney-Smythe is in his room, resting. You can't hope to remember anything if you stay here. You'll have to go out and about so that your memory can be prodded by the things you see."

The girl still looked troubled but she admitted, "Fraser, you are so full of good sense, and I am such a goose."

Fraser smiled as she dabbed a little more rouge on to Lucinda's cheeks. Then she handed the girl her bonnet and gloves.

"Go along now, my lady, and while you are gone I'll select some evening gowns for tonight and have them altered by the time you get back. There's sure to be one that takes your fancy."

"All of them, I expect," answered Lucinda with a laugh.

Expecting to slip out of the house unseen, she was a little taken aback at the sight of the earl and the countess in the hall as she approached the staircase. She hesitated on the topmost step as the pair paused in their conversation to look up at her, and only came forward when the countess said, "Ah, Lucinda, how much better you look today! Come along down, my dear."

If the countess's smile was a little strained, Lucinda was certain it was not on her account, for her tone had been cordial enough. But Lucinda still hesitated. She transferred her gaze, a little fearfully, to the earl whose expression was immediately transformed from one of inscrutability to one of admiration.

She lowered her eyes demurely as she continued down the stairs. She would have hated him to guess how his admiration of her appearance had thrilled her. What is more, it reassured her quite considerably. His strained behaviour on the one occasion he had visited her weighed heavily on her mind. He had acted in no way like a fond bridegroom, or even a worried one, and not being able to recall anything that had gone before, Lucinda had been somewhat distressed.

But now, it seemed, she had distorted that incident, for he took her hand and raised it slowly to his lips, saying, "You look extremely lovely, my dear. I am delighted to see you completely recovered."

The countess looked delighted and Lucinda considered herself fortunate to have a mother-in-law who was amiable in the extreme.

As the earl kissed her hand briefly Lucinda flushed and said, a little breathlessly, "I feel extremely hearty, but will only consider myself recovered when my memory returns, and," she added, laughing in a strained way, "I can be quite sure just who I am!"

The earl frowned suddenly and she was immediately sorry she had mentioned it. It must be, she realised, extremely galling for a man's wife to remember nothing of their life together.

He bowed stiffly, saying, "I must take my leave of you, ladies. If you will excuse me. . . ."

He moved away but was arrested immediately by his mother's voice. "You cannot go now, Dareth! Not on Lucinda's first day out of her bed."

Once more the earl could have throttled his mother but again his admirable self-control kept him in check.

"The weather is exceedingly clement," the countess went on quickly, avoiding looking directly at her son. "You and Lucinda could take a short stroll in the grounds."

Lucinda, who had been at that moment gazing at the magnificence around her in some awe, looked startled. The countess put her arm around her shoulder and pushed her gently towards her son. "Off you go you two. A short break from your work will do you much good also, Dareth."

Lucinda looked from the earl's furious countenance to his mother's smiling one. "I am sure," she said, her green eyes wide with alarm, "Dareth has much to occupy him."

Her use of his given name once more had an

odd effect on him. It was, of course, normally only the prerogative of those closest him, and he felt quite strange at having his name uttered by this young girl. And then, because he was reminded that she was an innocent victim of his mother's foolishness, he unbent quickly and said;

"There can be nothing of more importance to me than escorting you this morning."

He was rewarded by the smile of pleasure she bestowed upon him, so lacking in guile, and the light that shone out of her eyes. There could be no harm done in escorting the girl through the gardens for a while. There need be no pretence in showing her what she could not, in any event, have seen before. He would at least be spared reminiscing.

The countess made a sound that was something like a sigh of satisfaction, and then she said in that quick, breathless way which was so attractive, "Do not forget to put on your bonnet, my dear. The sun is quite strong for the time of year."

The earl stared hard at his mother, who pointedly ignored him, as Lucinda put on her chipstraw bonnet and tied the ribbons with shaking fingers. The moment she had finished, the earl abruptly turned and walked towards the door which was immediately opened by an alert footman, leaving Lucinda to hurry after him.

"Not too far, Dareth," his mother warned. "Remember, Lucinda has not quite recovered her strength yet."

The earl made no reply as he allowed Lucinda to procede him outside. "Perhaps as far as the Grecian temple . . ." she suggested.

Once outside the house Lucinda was far too self-conscious to notice the warmth of the day. The earl walked stiffly by her side, his hands clasped behind his back, his eyes fixed on some point directly ahead, and although he had, on second thoughts, shortened his stride to enable her to keep pace with him she was still finding it rather difficult to do so. Alone with him at last, Lucinda was miserably aware of the gulf between them and although she desperately sought for something to break the silence between them her tongue seemed firmly fixed in her mouth.

She cast a quick sideways glance at him. He was so big and alarming, his thoughts seemingly unwelcome ones if the forbidding set of his countenance was anything by which to judge. Lucinda could not imagine him tender and loving, and her cheeks flushed crimson at the unseemly trend of her own thoughts.

Quickly she transferred her attention to her surroundings once more. Before them lay acres and acres of green parkland which was natural in its appearance, yet bore the regularity only the hand of man could achieve. There were clumps of chestnut trees, an avenue of birches and elms. Oak trees spread their branches to envelop the birds which flitted continuously in and out of their leafy embrace.

Lucinda gazed around, gaining pleasure from all she saw. She took a deep breath of sweet, fresh air and could not help herself exclaiming, "How beautiful it all is. Such space, such light. Does it all belong to you, my lord?"

He paused momentarily, startled out of some very deep thoughts and stared at her. She wondered what had been occupying his mind to such an extent.

Suddenly he smiled and said, waving a hand to encompass all the eye could see, "All this, and a great deal more."

Lucinda flushed once more under his scrutiny, feeling he was somehow laughing at her. "You must think me a fool for asking such an elementary question."

"No," he answered, a mite sharply. "It has never been discussed between us before."

She eyed him curiously for a moment or two and then when it became apparent he intended to say no more on the subject she turned and scrutinised the house from a short distance away.

"It is," she said, determined not to endure another painful silence, "very large, is it not?"

"There are larger establishments." She did not look at him, for she knew his eyes were upon her and that there was a curious expression in them. "But," he added wryly, "they belong to various members of our royal family."

Lucinda laughed then and turned to look at him. Any tension there had been between them was gone like the bird who had just flown out of the eaves as they passed.

"I like it when you make me laugh."

He was still considering her thoughtfully. "I like it too when I make you laugh." And then he asked briskly, "Shall we walk a little further?"

She hurried to join him as they set off down a narrow path. "One of these days I should like just to sit and count the windows. I should say there are at least two hundred of them. Perhaps even more."

He allowed himself a quick glance at her but did not slow his pace. "There are two hundred and fifty-six."

"Oh, you shouldn't have told me! Now it will be no fun counting."

He looked mildly amused at her idle chatter. "There will be far more important matters for your attention."

"Not if the last few days are anything by which to judge. I find it difficult to allow someone to do everything for me. I am not making a very admirable countess."

He drew a sharp breath and Lucinda was aware again of a withdrawal in him. She wondered if it had been caused by her indirect mention of her accident. Even so, his abrupt changes of mood towards her were as puzzling as they were distressing.

"Tell me something of its history," she said breathlessly, hoping to restore his good humour and the ease with which they had been conversing.

Her plea had the desired effect of diverting him. The path down which they were walking was a narrow one, lined with luxuriant trees which drew her eyes frequently. Box hedges edged the path itself and they were alive with wild flowers of myriad colours. Lucinda could not see over them and so it seemed as if they were separated from the rest of the world. The flowers in the hedges fascinated her. Whilst never allowing her attention to wander from him for a moment, she paused now and then to admire a flower or a bush.

"Glenbrooke Abbey," the earl told her, "was built by Jeremiah Farringdon who was a courtier of Henry the Eighth." He glanced at her and smiled wryly, which did strange things to her calm. "He was sometimes known as the king's executioner because of his willingness to dispose of quietly anyone who had fallen foul of his king."

She gasped. "How horrible. Fraser did mention the man to me, but I cannot believe you have such an infamous relative. Is the story true?"

"It *is* only a story," mused the earl, "but such stories usually have an ounce of truth in them. In any event, it is likely that my ancestor was not of a kindly disposition. It is certain he was a favourite of the king, and the king's favour was never lightly earned. Eventually, in recognition of whatever services Jeremiah performed, King Henry bestowed on him the title Earl of Glenbrooke, and gave him this considerable estate which has been, down the years, gradually added to. Eventually, Jeremiah took a wealthy wife and as far as it is known he lived happily ever after."

"I don't know how his conscience allowed him to do so," she murmured. Some late-flowering almond blossom still clung to some of the trees and she pulled down a low branch so as to inhale the perfume. She looked at him wide-eyed as she let the branch go again. "Is it true that the king resided in my room?"

"The reason we have a room fit for the king is because it was obligatory for any courtier to have one just in case the monarch did decide to pay a visit. My forefather provided an extremely handsome one as you have seen but there is no evidence, sad to say, to suggest the king actually did stay here at any time, although, of course, the possibility does remain."

"I am most disappointed," she admitted. "I had hoped to have slept in his bed." She laughed self-consciously a moment later. "I did not mean it to sound quite like that."

He stopped and smiled at her in her confusion. "I'm sorry if you are disappointed, but it is possible that Queen Anne may have spent one night here, almost one hundred years ago. That is in doubt too, but more of a possibility nevertheless. Does that make you feel happier?"

She flashed him an answering smile. "Much." She glanced at him anxiously as they resumed their walk. "You must find my endless quizzing tiresome. Pray do not be afraid to tell me to stop, for I chatter far too much when left unchecked."

"By no means," he answered heartily. "It is quite a pleasure to show Glenbrooke Abbey to someone who has never seen it before, and someone who is so genuinely interested."

She murmured, "You are too kind," and then, "Why is it called Glenbrooke Abbey? It surely isn't an abbey."

"The original abbey of Glenbrooke lies three miles across the fields on my land. When Henry dissolved the monasteries he distributed much of the land attached to them amongst his favourites. The first earl built his house where it is because the view is a better one. The abbey, itself, after being stripped and desecrated, fell to ruin. There are but a few stones left." He glanced at her. "You may visit the site when you are stronger, but it is much too far for you to go just now."

His concern was touching and Lucinda was very moved by it. The path had come almost to a Grecian temple situated on a slight rise of the land, to give unparalleled views of the surrounding countryside.

"How delightful!" she exclaimed. "How pleasant it must be to sit here in such peaceful surroundings and survey the countryside."

"Would you care to do so now?" asked the earl. "You may well need a rest before making the return journey to the house. We have walked a fair distance."

She was flustered again by such concern. She wished she could accept it gracefully, but felt it was something she had never enjoyed before.

"It does not seem like it. I have enjoyed every moment of our walk," she answered, suddenly breathless.

He took her hand and led her across the small strip of grass which surrounded the temple. Once inside he handed her to a seat and after only a moment's hesitation sat down beside her. Lucinda folded her hands demurely in her lap and gazed about her, her eyes bright with the pleasure of all she saw; the fields in the distance where the farmers toiled to make the best of the weather, the trees where the larks sang their sweet song, and the profusion of early summer flowers all around the temple.

Perhaps, she mused, her loss of memory was the real cause, but the scenery around her, the earl's presence at her side, gave her a feeling of total unreality. She felt she would have to hold tightly on to all those beloved images, lest she might lose them completely.

Nearby a deep stream gurgled its way over stones and as she caught sight of it, Lucinda gave a little gasp.

The earl, who had been looking at her, said, "Is something amiss? You seem distressed. I fear we may have walked too far after all, and the sun is quite strong."

"No, it is not that." She could not look at him. "The stream. Isn't that where ... ?"

He sighed heavily. "So you have heard. Yes, that is where my father was drowned, but not, you will be relieved to hear, at this precise spot. It is further downstream that it becomes much deeper. Even so, my mother will no longer come here although the temple was erected for her only three years ago. Before the accident she spent many an hour here enjoying the view just as you are doing."

Lucinda looked at him then, her eyes filled with pain; her concern was for him only. "I was most sorry to hear of it, Dareth."

His lips twisted into a bitter smile. "No doubt you have also heard the rumour that followed hard on my father's death."

"Yes," she answered, "but I do not understand why it was said of you. You would have no reason to do such a thing."

"Presumably it would be to gain control of the estate. To me it seems a paltry motive, but to some it is obviously enough."

"It's abominable that anyone should consider you capable...."

She broke off in embarrassment. The bitter smile remained on his lips. "Do you find it so hard to believe?"

"Of course," she answered hotly.

"I assure you there are many who do not."

"No one who knows you in the least could ever believe that such stories are more than malicious gossip!"

She looked so indignant that he stared at her in amazement and then she added in some confusion, "You are, I have noted, inordinately fond of your mother. You would not cause her pain whatever the gain to yourself, and I am certain I should not have associated with you if you were not a man of the greatest honour. Besides, Dareth, it is quite inconceivable to anyone of any sensibility that you could be guilty of any humbug whatsoever."

In the face of such an impassioned declaration the earl could only stare in astonishment. And then, as her eyes searched his face, eyes completely without guile, he was filled with guilt and remorse. They were, much to his discomfort, two emotions that had assailed him with unaccustomed frequency of late.

He took her hand in his. "Oh, Lucy," was all he could find to say after a moment. "How misplaced is your trust in me."

He was far from being an innocent, but never before had he met a girl who was so unworldly. She trusted anyone who spoke to her kindly, and just then it was unbearable.

She stared down at the hands he grasped in his lean, brown ones, and then gently she disentangled them. She got to her feet slowly and went to stand against one of the marble pillars of the temple. If he was guilty of such infamy she didn't want to know of it, but she was sure she could not be mistaken in her judgement of him. Perhaps as she feared he had not married her for love, and she was certainly undecided as to her feelings for him, but he was not a wicked man, of that she was quite convinced.

"Am I usually addressed as Lucy?" she asked a moment later, keeping her back towards him. "It is rather silly to admit I do not know my own name."

There was a moment's silence, during which she dared not turn round, and then he answered, "It is *my* name for you."

She whirled round, twisting her hands together in anguish. "This is so terribly unfair on you, Dareth. I feel I must talk of it now while we are alone, for I am quite certain you will not speak of it to me."

The earl became alert and she went on quickly, before he could interrupt, "While I am still without memory of anything that occurred between us before I came here, it is inconceivable that we can recapture any degree of . . . closeness in our relationship. . . ." He got to his feet in alarm and she turned away again, pulling the shawl closer around her shoulders, for she felt suddenly cold and more than a little frightened. "So if you wish us to part, I beg of you, only say so."

He came across to her and rested his hands

lightly on her shoulders for a mere moment. Then he let them fall to his sides again. There seemed to be an unending silence between them.

When at last he found his voice it was harsh. "There is no point in discussing the matter at this time, Lucy. You have only today got up from your sick bed."

"I feel quite recovered. I do not think I am a weakling, but it shall be as you wish. I shall be pleased to discuss the matter whenever you deem it time to do so." She turned to face him once more, forcing a smile to her face. "Shall we walk back now? I am beginning to feel fatigued."

The downstairs sitting room had been cleaned and aired to accommodate those guests at Glenbrooke Abbey who might wish to stroll through the French windows into the formal gardens while the present fine spell lasted.

The earl and Lucinda returned to the house by way of the formal gardens, stopping frequently so that she could admire this bush or that flower, which, to his embarrassment, the earl could not identify. He was becoming rather exasperated with the girl. Surely she could not expect him to be knowledgeable about a *garden* when he employed an army of gardeners to tend it for him? But, to his chagrin, Lucinda did.

Whilst the earl and Lucinda had been about their walk, Melissa, her husband and brother-in-law had returned from their visiting and were, together with the countess, enjoying tea. A table had been set out on the paved terrace where the profusion of trees all around ensured there could not be the slightest exposure to the sun, and there was also a degree of protection from any breeze that might suddenly spring up.

The earl, since leaving the Grecian temple, had been suffering for the first time in his life, from a severely troubled conscience, which added to the small irritation he was feeling towards Lucinda, and seeing Digby Stacey partaking of tea so contentedly whilst enjoying the earl's reluctant hospitality did nothing to improve his humour.

It was much to his relief, however, that Lucinda's ironic offer to free him had not, apparently, dampened her spirits to any degree, for she had been in quite a good humour during their walk back. But on seeing so many strangers waiting to meet her she hesitated and became shy again. She stopped under the rose arbour, clutching at a bunch of forget-me-nots and violets which she had collected on the way back.

When he realised she was no longer at his side the earl paused and glanced back at her. "Come along," he said in a soft voice. "Why do you wait there?"

"Shall I not be intruding?" she asked.

He laughed. "How can that be so? They have been waiting most impatiently to meet you."

He held out his hand and, giving him a smile, she took it readily, and they continued along the path to the house. As they approached Sir Hugo and his brother shot to their feet. Without realising it, the earl gripped Lucinda's hand even tighter. The countess looked up sharply as she heard them approach. She looked troubled for a moment and then, when she realised nothing was amiss, and quite the contrary was the case, she relaxed again and set out two dishes for the newcomers.

"Oh, how glad I am to meet you!" exclaimed Melissa, rushing forward to clutch at a rather astonished Lucinda.

"The delight is mutual," murmured the girl shyly when she was at last released.

The earl rescued her from his sister and led her, a little more confidently now, towards his other guests. "Sir Hugo Stacey, my brother-in-law," said the earl. "Allow me to introduce. . . ." He was about to say, Miss Lucinda Kendricks, but only just in time checked himself and said instead, simply, "Lucinda."

Sir Hugo bowed stiffly and took her hand. Stiffening slightly, the earl said, "And Lieutenant Stacey. Sir Hugo's brother, lately returned from the Peninsula where he has been causing Bonaparte no small amount of trouble."

The earl was fully aware that since their arrival Digby Stacey had been staring, almost rudely, in astonishment at Lucinda. When she smiled at him he stirred himself and bowed low over her hand.

"I am most honoured to make your ladyship's acquaintance."

"And I you, Lieutenant Stacey," she answered with a degree of style which astonished the earl. Involuntarily he glanced at his mother who smiled wryly and then looked away again.

"I am given to understand you are a hero," Lucinda went on. "I am most honoured to know you, sir."

The earl's earlier irritation returned. It seemed the girl was actually impressed by his pretty speech and by the man himself.

The lieutenant now, reluctantly, drew his attention away from Lucinda and glanced slyly at the earl. "No wonder you kept her a secret, old boy. With this beauty you did well to make sure of no rival for her hand."

Dareth checked his impatience at the obvious allusion to what must now be his well-known failure to gain Caroline Kingsley's hand. It was fortunate just then that Melissa said, "How right you are, Digby. When I heard Dareth was married I admit I feared the type of wife he might have chosen. You've no idea what a relief it is to me to find it is you, Lucinda, and yet I should have known. Dareth has always had such very good taste."

The earl stiffened slightly and was finding it difficult to keep a pleasant expression on his face. As to his mother, she had to keep her head averted and her son knew she was trying hard not to laugh. And Lucinda herself looked suitably bemused at such a sudden onslaught of compliments.

"Come, sit by me," Melissa invited, "so we can get to know each other with no further delay. I just know we shall be the best of friends, and being newly married you may benefit from my experience."

Lucinda was glad to obey Dareth's sister, who was no more alarming than was his mother. Melissa's inane chatter was just the thing to divert her mind. Her walk with the earl had unnerved her considerably despite her conscious attempt to appear nonchalant.

The earl withdrew a little to the furthermost seat and, folding his arms, settled down to view the proceedings. His mother beamed happily in his direction but he affected not to notice it, and she turned back to Lucinda, saying, "Do give me those flowers before they droop. Walsingham can put them in a little water and take them to your room. How pretty they are."

The earl frowned slightly as the lieutenant moved his chair closer to Lucinda and proceeded to engage her in conversation whilst Melissa paused in hers to sip at her tea.

"I do hope Uncle Percival will be down soon," she said putting her dish down. "He is as impatient to make Lucinda's acquaintance as I was."

Much to Lieutenant Stacey's annoyance Melissa turned back to Lucinda then. "We were all grieved to hear of your accident, dearest. How dreadfully provoking it must be not to be able to remember *anything*. I cannot imagine not knowing my own husband."

Lucinda's ready smile died. She stared down at her hands which were clasped demurely in her lap. "It is more provoking by far for Dareth, I fear."

Unable to contain himself a moment longer, the earl got to his feet abruptly and said in a harsher tone of voice than he had intended to use, "Lucy, you'd best go to your room and rest before dinner. It has been a tiring day for you."

"Ah, such a considerate bridegroom," said Digby Stacey, a trace of mockery very evident in his voice. "This is quite a new facet to your character, Glenbrooke."

The earl managed to force a smile to his face. "It is hardly a facet *you* would enjoy, Stacey."

"Lucinda shall not leave us yet," insisted Melissa. "We have only just become acquainted."

"Lucy cannot answer your endless quizzing," her brother warned, trying not to become out of patience, and Lucinda herself merely looked confused, not knowing whether to stay or go.

The matter was decided a moment later with the arrival on the scene of Percival Courtney-Smythe. He ambled out of the sitting room, leaning heavily on his cane and breathing in a laboured way. He glanced around and clapped eyes on Lucinda.

"My dear, I cannot tell you how delighted I am that you are so much better. Why, you look as if nothing has been wrong with you! Allow me, as the eldest member of this family, to welcome you as the newest."

Lucinda smiled prettily and he added, glancing up at the sky. "I am sure it is with the best intentions that everyone has allowed you to remain out here, my dear, but in view of your recent confinement to bed it is extremely undesirable. Come, take my arm, and we will sit inside a while, and you must tell me all about yourself."

It was the countess who stood up first. "Uncle Percival, what can Lucinda possibly tell you? As you already know she has no memory. It will only distress her to be quizzed endlessly."

Great Uncle Percival sniffed loudly and puffed out his huge stomach even further. "I'll not tire the child, never you fear, Adeline. It's just a coze I'm wanting. Come along, my dear."

Lucinda shot the earl an imploring glance and then did as she was told. Percival Courtney-Smythe turned his attention to Melissa then, and peering at the girl, said, "It is sheer folly for a woman in your condition to be exposed to the elements."

Melissa giggled shyly and exchanged loving looks with her spouse. "And," added her great-uncle, "you must sit on a higher chair, if you are hoping for a boy. Isn't that so, Adeline?"

"Oh, indeed," answered the countess.

"Nonsense," said Melissa firmly and then, looking at her great uncle, "Dareth and Lucinda met whilst he was exercising his cattle on Hampstead

Heath, Great Uncle Percival. Isn't that the most romantic thing you have ever heard?"

The countess looked provoked beyond bearing, which gave her son some grim satisfaction. She was now beginning to experience some of his own exasperation, and, as he well knew, it could only grow worse. With every day that passed they would pass deeper into the maze of deceit until it was impossible to find any way out.

Digby Stacey was looking at him from beneath a pair of drooping lids. "I had no idea you frequented the Heath with those admirable animals of yours."

"How could you?" retorted the earl. "You never go there yourself."

He followed with his eyes the departing figures of Lucinda and his great uncle. He watched his worried mother usher Melissa after them.

He then transferred his attention to Digby Stacey once more, annoyed that he should have to speak to him at all, let alone explain. "Fortunately, as you will agree, I took the occasional turn about the Heath. And as you have already said, I took care with Lucy not to invite rivals for her hand."

His more urbane manner had returned suddenly as he realised the fop had taken a great shine to his "wife." He was beginning to enjoy this aspect of the situation.

"I have a new curricle you and Sir Hugo might like to inspect. I suggest we adjourn to the coach house and leave the ladies and my great uncle to their gossiping."

Sir Hugo, who had been contemplating the shine on his boots with great concentration, jumped to his feet. "What a splendid idea, Glenbrooke. Domesticity, admirable as it is, becomes rather wearing after a time."

The earl raised a quizzical eye at the younger Stacey who was rather more reluctant to agree. He was looking a mite regretfully into the sitting room where Lucinda and Percival Courtney-Smythe were cosily ensconced.

"Yes, yes, by all means, Glenbrooke," he answered a moment later. "I am about to order a new conveyance myself."

Chapter Seven

The countess turned and smiled with pleasure when, a few nights later, her son entered her dressing room as she prepared to go down for dinner.

"It's nice to see you, dearest," she murmured, turning back to her mirror to inspect the confection of feathers adorning her hair. "We seem to have had so little chance of late to be private with each other. But," she added, standing further away from the mirror so as to obtain a better view of her appearance, "it is so delightful having the house full again, and especially nice to have Melissa and Hugo here."

She turned to face him, holding out her hands. He took them in his own and raised them to his lips. "You are looking quite splendid tonight."

She dimpled. "Do you really think so? I thought puce was a mite insipid for me, but perhaps you and Fraser are right. I am liking it more now I am growing used to it."

The earl glanced towards the door to the bed-chamber. "Where is the good woman?"

The countess's eyes widened slightly. "Fraser?" She smiled. "She is with Lucinda, helping her to dress for dinner." She gazed at him fondly. "You have been good with her, dearest, and I am so grateful to you, but," she added, sighing and drawing away her hands, "I did not fully comprehend how difficult this matter would become. I live in fear that any day her memory may return, for her sake just as well as your own. That it will be damaging enough to us is sure, but I have grown quite fond of the chit. She is such an engaging child. Uncle Percival finds her so too. He has hardly allowed her from his side in days. I don't know what they can find to talk about."

A light seemed to have been extinguished from the earl's eyes too. "That is what I have come to discuss with you, Mother."

"Matters will grow easier tomorrow. Melissa and Sir Hugo have planned to leave and Uncle Percival has sent word to his housekeeper to make preparations for *his* return, so this farce will come to an end before long. I confess it was wise of you to refuse any celebrations for your birthday. We would have been entertaining for days, and I just cannot face up to it at the moment."

The earl sank down on to the chaise longue. As he did so he straightened his exquisitely cut dark blue evening coat so that it did not crease, and said in heartfelt tones, "You cannot imagine how relieved your news has made me, Mother." He brought out his snuff box and took a pinch. "I am sure I could not abide another single day of Melissa's effusions over Miss Kendricks. How delighted she is to have such a sweet sister-in-law and how she hopes we too will have exciting news to bestow before long."

The countess gave a quick sharp shout of laughter which she stifled when her son flashed her a quelling look.

"It is only to be expected, dearest," she said gently.

He ran one hand through his carefully arrayed locks, which only served to put them to further disorder. "Great Uncle Percival actually had the effrontery to congratulate me on my choice of bride. He said," the earl went on in outraged tones, "he hadn't expected me to choose so wisely."

The countess made no attempt to stifle her laughter on this occasion. "He is excessively taken with her, Dareth. It really is all we could have wished for."

He eyed her coldly. "And is Stacey's lickspittle way all you could have wished for too, Mother? He has been at her side like a confounded lapdog since the moment he clapped eyes on her."

The countess went off into further peals of laughter. "I cannot see why you are so annoyed,

Dareth. I know you dislike him, and his style is a mite . . . bizarre, but you said quite clearly you did not wish for her company, so you should have no cause for complaint. You have been able to go about your business and no one has thought odd of it."

The earl nodded. "I certainly have brought myself up to date on a great many matters of estate business since our visitors arrived; matters even my father never concerned himself with. My cause for complaint is certainly not on my own behalf, but on Luc . . . Miss Kendricks'."

His mother, who had cast him an amused glance at the use of her name, looked troubled now. "Oh, Dareth, how can we tell her? I do believe Uncle Percival will leave here hard on the heels of Melissa and Sir Hugo. There will be nothing to keep her here then. I don't know how to tell Melissa you and Lucinda have parted. She will take it very hard, I fear, and I shall be instrumental in hurting her."

The earl got to his feet; his face was a grim mask. He took out his watch and glanced at it before consigning it back to his pocket.

"We have time," his mother said, her eyes surveying him curiously. She was rarely puzzled as to his moods, but tonight she was uncertain as to his humour. "The others will be some time yet."

"It will be your task to tell Melissa what you will when the time comes, but I shall tell . . . Miss

Kendricks as soon as Great Uncle Percival has left. . . ."

"I shall not be able to face her."

He smiled grimly. "I fancy she will not want to face *us*." He turned round. "Our original plan will have to be amended."

The countess's eyes opened wide. "What plan, dearest?"

The earl gave a gasp of exasperation. His mother had never seen him look so tense.

"When this began you said you would obtain a post for Miss Kendricks with a respectable family."

"Oh, that plan! You can be sure I have already made discreet enquiries."

"Well, it won't do." His tone was sharp.

"What *do* you mean, Dareth?"

"This past se'ennight, Mother, Lucy has been accorded all the honour due to my wife. The servants have bowed and curtsied to her, fetched and carried for her, and she was worn clothes the like of which she has never seen before. All this is quite aside from my sister's compliments which she has showered upon Lucy, Great Uncle Percival's attention, and," he made a grimace of disapproval, "not the least, Digby Stacey's adoration. In short, Lucy truly believes she is a countess and she will grow more used to the way of life as each day passes."

"What do you suggest, dearest?"

His mother was very uncertain as to how to

treat him in such an odd mood, and therefore went very warily.

"We cannot expect her to revert to a life of servitude after all she has enjoyed beneath this roof. It will be hurtful enough for her to discover she is not after all the Countess of Glenbrooke, and heaven knows I do not relish having to tell her that. She will have to be at the beck and call of some peevish female for the remainder of her days, and that will be beyond bearing." He looked hard at his mother. "You will have to find her a husband."

For one incredulous moment the countess was devoid of speech and then she clapped her hands together delightedly. "What a splendid idea, Dareth! How I wish I could have conceived such an idea myself."

She began to pace the floor, one finger to her lips. "Let me but think a moment. Who can we find, I wonder?"

"Is it necessary to think of someone just now?"

But his mother was not listening. She laughed triumphantly. "I know, Dareth. Fencham. Fencham will be perfect for her."

"Who on earth is Fencham?"

"The third footman." She waved her hand in the air. "He only came to us three months ago but Latimer assures me he is most satisfactory. He is, as yet, unmarried, I collect. And you have a cottage free at Raston. They can live there. And, of course, she will be allowed to keep all Melissa's clothes. Fencham is an extremely handsome young man. He will do admirably."

"He may be an Adonis," answered her son vexedly, "but he won't do either."

"Why won't he do, pray tell me?"

"Miss Kendricks, for the very same reasons I've mentioned already, cannot marry a servant any more than she can become one now."

It was now the countess's turn to look vexed. "I think, dearest, you are fast losing sight of who and what Miss Kendricks really is. She is as charming a girl as one would wish to meet, but marrying even a third footman is more than she could have looked forward to less than a fortnight ago."

"That may be true, Mother, but Lucy is now what we, heaven forgive us, have made of her."

The countess put one hand over her breast and stared at her son incredulously. "Dareth," she said in a less than steady voice, "you do not mean to marry her yourself."

His manner became even more frosty. "It would be the most honourable thing to do. Surely you cannot argue with that? She has been most horribly compromised by this business."

"No one but we know of it," she answered faintly. "She is not about to marry into Society so it cannot make any difference to her prospects."

"Would you find it so abhorrent if I were to marry her?" The countess shook her head, shock having rendered her speechless. "You need have no fear on that score, Mother," he said scathingly a moment or two later.

She looked up at her son, her breathing becoming more steady. "You do not mean to marry her?"

His lips tightened into a grim line. "What I intend is for her to make a good match."

The countess sank down on to the chaise longue and waved her hand towards the dresser. "My vinaigrette, Dareth, if you please. I feel quite faint."

He found the bottle quickly and handed it to her, anxious now. "Are you all right, dearest?"

She nodded as she clutched the bottle in her hand. "I am sorry, Mother, if I alarmed you. I didn't mean to do so. Shall I have Fraser summoned to attend you?"

Her hand dropped to her side and she shook her head. Her son gently eased her back into the cushions of the chaise longue.

"There will be no necessity for anyone to be summoned on my behalf," she said a moment later. "But I am sure this business will be the end of me." She sought out her son's hand and clasped it tightly in her own. "And before you say I am deserving of it. . . ."

"I wouldn't dream of saying so, Mama."

". . . I have been a foolish and unfeeling woman. You are quite right about Lucinda. We must do what we can for the child. We have used her abominably. Why, she has even suggested changes in the running of the house which I believe will be for the best."

The earl settled back beside his mother and she said, recovering suddenly, "I do believe I have an idea."

"Not another one," answered her weary son, and when the countess looked at him she saw that his eyes were filled with amusement, much to her relief. His acceptance these past days of the situation in which she had placed them, had not only relieved her enormously, but had troubled her too. On reflection she realised it was quite unlike her son to submit so readily to such an imposition.

"Lieutenant Stacey," she said in triumph, watching him anxiously for his reaction.

"What about Stacey?" he asked sharply.

"He is absolutely besotted by her. Even Melissa has commented upon it, and they have been in each other's company almost constantly for the best part of a week."

"He believes her to be my wife."

The countess laughed gaily, casting aside so trivial a point. "When he learns that after all she is not, he will be too relieved to question further. He will regard it as one of your larks, as indeed we shall have to call it. And I do believe Lucinda has a marked partiality for him too. She was most impressed by his military record. They deal very well together. They talk endlessly."

The earl's face was an uncompromising mask of grimness. Those facts had not escaped him. "Do they indeed," he murmured. He stood up in a very abrupt manner. "Well, it won't do."

"Dareth! I do believe you are forgetting the circumstances of this matter."

"Never," he retorted angrily. "Lucy cannot be taken with a fop such as Digby Stacey. I refuse to believe it."

"Let me remind you, my boy, Digby Stacey is much sought after as a likely husband, and deservedly so. He is a pleasant enough young man. . . ."

"But his affectations, Mother, and his sense of style!"

"Faugh! As if Lucinda would consider that a detriment. The Staceys are a respectable and well-placed family. A girl even of the highest birth would be glad of an alliance with them, including your own sister."

The earl drew out his watch again. "Time is passing, Mother." He put it back in his pocket. "Miss Kendricks," he said stiffly, "may choose whom she pleases. Hugo will ensure Stacey remains silent on this matter as it affects their family honour too, so I have no fears on that score, but I doubt if the lieutenant would regard Lucy as a fit wife since she has been compromised so much. Besides, Lieutenant Stacey may not find her quite so attractive when he learns she is not my wife. I fear much of her attraction lies in the fact he believes her to belong to me.

"I shall provide a portion for her but I am also

persuaded that for a second son unable to return to his military career, it will not be sufficient."

"You are quite mistaken on every score, Dareth. He is so taken with her I wager it will be of no significance. However, I shall not scruple to argue with you over it. But, pray tell me, how we are to give her a choice of partners of whom *you* will approve?"

The earl drew himself up sharply. "In view of this . . . matter being caused by you, Mother, it will fall to you, in the autumn, after instructing Miss Kendricks in the genteel arts, to escort her to London. You can explain her presence as best you can. No one will question her background too closely, for under your patronage she will be ensured of social success and her own demeanour will ensure she attracts an offer or two from respectable persons." He leaned forward slightly. "It is the very least we can do for her."

"Oh, certainly," agreed his mother, her eyes wide with wonder. "It's quite the best idea yet. I shall love to launch her into Society, to supervise her wardrobe and plan everything just as I did for your sister. I had not thought to do it again."

The earl looked suitably pleased at the reception of his plan. His mother chuckled suddenly. "I may even present her at Court. It will be such a lark, gammoning Society. Seeing those so puffed up by their own consequence paying homage to our little orphan girl. I don't wonder, if I put my mind to it, she'll snare a duke!"

"Mother!"

At the warning note in his voice, she looked recalcitrant. "Never worry, dearest; I have learned my lesson on this occasion."

"I sincerely hope so," answered her son in heartfelt tones, and, going over to the door of the dressing room he added, "We are late for dinner, my dear."

As she hurried over to take his arm she went on excitedly, "And much as I would love to supervise a social season for Lucinda, I admit it still would be best if she were to be settled before that. I cannot understand why you are so against Lieutenant Stacey." She glanced up at him slyly but his face was an expressionless mask. "I still believe the matter *will* be settled once Stacey learns he need hold back no longer."

Determined to have the last word, the earl replied, "And I refuse to believe Miss Kendricks has such low taste."

Chapter Eight

It was late the following morning that Lucinda found both the upstairs drawing room and the downstairs sitting room empty of people.

For almost a full week she had grown accustomed to not being able to wander around the house without meeting someone who insisted on bearing her company. Usually it was Melissa, who talked gaily of her first and only London season during which she had met and married Sir Hugo, and she talked of her life as the mistress of Stockley Hall, which sounded a grand establishment, and of her excitement at the prospect of becoming a mother. This morning Lucinda and Melissa had bid each other an emotional farewell followed by fervent promises of frequent visits in the future.

Very often, when he was not resting, Great Uncle Percival would insist that Lucinda sit with him and talk with him, and it gave her great pleasure to do so. She found Lieutenant Stacey's company enjoyable too, although she sensed that he and the earl were not too friendly. Lucinda could not find fault with his manner of address, and was both surprised and flattered by his constant attention and frequent compliments about her every word and act. He accompanied her whenever she decided to stroll in the garden, and engineered a place near to her of an evening in the drawing room after dinner. He had even attempted to teach her to play chess until she admitted no liking for the game. Lucinda had a clear preference for such games as faro and whist, and surprised everyone by winning each time either was played. Lieutenant Stacey, she was aware, did not approve of such unladylike pursuits as billiards, but encouraged by the earl, who seemed to derive a great deal of amusement from the way she tackled every challenge, she often joined the men when they retired to the billiards room. She was quite hurt however when they refused to allow her to join their shooting party two days ago. She had, reluctantly, remained behind to bear Great Uncle Percival company, much to the old man's delight, whilst Melissa and the countess went shopping for materials in Leicester.

Lucinda had grown very fond of the people of Glenbrooke Abbey, and was grateful that none of them, not even the countess, made an issue of her lost memory, which showed no sign of an immediate return.

Even though Lucinda concentrated her thoughts

very hard, there was not even a glimmer of remembrance, although her loss of memory did not curtail her enjoyment of her stay at Glenbrooke Abbey. She entered into every activity whole-heartedly, gaining the admiration of both the men and the women, and she was sure she had never enjoyed herself so much. And the admiration she saw in the earl's eyes every time she won at cards or at billiards thrilled her.

And yet her conviction that she was not used to so luxurious a life remained with her and could not be dispelled however hard she tried. Nor could her uneasiness on behalf of the earl.

She saw him regularly, of course. Although she usually missed his presence at breakfast or luncheon, he was always present for dinner and was as attentive as Great Uncle Percival's and the Staceys' presence allowed him to be. But it was no more than that. He was still as much of a stranger as ever, and even though his words and manner were cordial enough there was nothing warmer in his attitude towards her, and he had not sought to speak to her privately since their walk in the grounds days ago.

Lucinda appreciated he was busy on estate business, as the countess had explained, and he needs must show attentiveness to his guests, but, she reasoned, they were after all recently wed and she badly needed reassurance on that score. If only, she thought time and time again, she could but recall their relationship before the accident. But try as she would, it was impossible.

The fact that she could not remember did not, however, prevent her from starting violently each time someone knocked on the door of the bed-chamber. Usually it was a servant with hot water, or cocoa, or Fraser with freshly laundered linen. (Lucinda could not help herself wondering at the vast amount available for her use). And occasionally it would be the countess, come to bid her good night. On no occasion was it the earl.

Lucinda sank down forlornly in to a chair placed near to one of the open windows. A robin hopped happily from branch to branch in a nearby cherry tree, but this morning Lucinda refused to be charmed by his merry song.

She stared mournfully out into the colourful gardens. In the past few days she had discovered a talent for arranging flowers prettily in vases and, although the gardeners voiced their disapproval of her collecting armfuls of blooms, the countess had encouraged her to do many arrangements which now were displayed about the house.

After Lucinda had been staring unseeingly ahead for some few minutes she was roused by the sound of uneven steps on the path outside. She stiffened slightly, and then relaxed again when she realised it could not possibly be the earl. Uncon-sciously, over the past few days, she had become aware of him whenever he approached, and she could now easily recognise his sure step.

A figure appeared in the opening of the window. "Lady Glenbrooke," said Lieutenant Stacey, "I have been hoping to see you."

He came further into the room and she was glad he no longer blocked out the sunlight. She loved to feel it on her face, even though the countess had expressed horror at such a partiality, and Lucinda admired the countess. But even she had to admit that it had put a becoming bloom on Lucinda's cheeks.

Lieutenant Stacey was dressed as always in the most fashionable mode, although to Lucinda he was nowhere near as elegant as the earl. In fact, whenever the earl was in the company of other men she always considered him to be superior in every way by comparison.

"Why, Lieutenant Stacey," she said when she had recovered from her surprise. "I did not look to see you here. I thought you gone with Sir Hugo and Lady Stacey."

He held a single rose bloom in his hand which he presented to her. She blushed slightly as she accepted it, still unable to respond to such gestures as serenely as she wished.

"I could not possibly leave here without taking my leave of you, Lady Glenbrooke."

Lucinda's pink cheeks took on a deeper hue. "You honour me, sir."

"No," he assured her, laughing heartily, "the honour is all mine." He took her hand and raised it to his lips. "We shall not yet be forced to say our goodbyes, my lady, for which I am most thankful. Every minute I am in your company is a golden one to be treasured."

Lucinda guessed she was becoming accustomed to his lavish compliments, for they failed to affect her as they had done several days ago.

"You have decided to stay on, Lieutenant Stacey?"

He smiled slightly. "Not here, Lady Glenbrooke, but with some friends who live but three miles from here. They were quite surprised to hear of your marriage to Glenbrooke, for the news of it had not reached them."

She smiled. "It is no use my commenting, Lieutenant Stacey. As you are well aware, I have no memory of anything prior to last week."

For once he did not return her smile. He was gazing at her in an unnaturally severe manner. "I cannot help but think, Lady Glenbrooke, that it is a great pity," he said at last.

"Oh, indeed," she admitted. "One is so limited by a memory which goes back only a matter of days."

"May I sit down?"

"Please do, Lieutenant Stacey," Lucinda agreed hurriedly. "I have been remiss in not inviting you earlier. Does your leg still pain you?"

He smiled slightly, enjoying her concern. His injured leg had considerably improved his popularity with the opposite sex.

"Only a little, Lady Glenbrooke."

"I fear it was a grievous injury that you make little of."

The lieutenant drew a sigh as he straightened his cuff. "It will never be quite the same as before, but, my physician tells me, it should improve considerably with time, and trouble me but a little."

Lucinda looked at him pityingly. "What a dreadful war it is, to be sure."

"Yes, indeed, Lady Glenbrooke."

"Shall we ever get the better of Bonaparte, do you think?"

"I am certain of it, my lady. Sir Arthur is an able commander, and his men most valiant."

Lucinda dimpled. "I am fully aware of *that*, Lieutenant Stacey." She sank back into the cushions. "The countess—my mother-in-law—spent her honeymoon trip in Europe, which was before the Terror, you will recall. She says that even if Bonaparte is defeated, France will never be the same country it was."

"I fear she is right," agreed the lieutenant.

Lucinda looked at him questioningly a moment or two later. "It has occurred to me, Lieutenant Stacey, that you and the earl are not on the best of terms, and I am at a loss to understand why."

The lieutenant smiled superciliously. "The earl and I are of different dispositions. . . ."

She laughed and the lieutenant was not at all sure he liked the tone of it. "Yes, I have noticed!"

He was vexed but he hastened to hide it from

the woman who had unwittingly stolen his heart. "The earl, I regret to say, belongs to a fast set, Lady Glenbrooke." Her smile faded. "They are reckless beyond belief, and nothing is beyond them. During the past few days I have been privileged to know you, my lady, and I feel sure that if you knew Glenbrooke well you would not have married him.

"I have been fortunate in being able to fight for my country. If it were possible I would return to do it further services. Some young men—the earl amongst them—stay at home and do nothing but dissipate their time. There is bound to be friction between us."

"Should you be saying this to me, Lieutenant Stacey?" Lucinda asked in a gentle voice.

He refused to look at her. "Forgive me, my lady, I did not mean to speak so bluntly, but it seems that someone should tell you certain things. It appears to me you have been kept in blissful ignorance."

He looked markedly discomforted but for her sake he was determined to go on. "The circumstances of your marriage."

"The circumstances are ordinary enough, Lieutenant Stacey," she answered mildly. Nevertheless, she was uneasy. "Secret weddings are common enough occurrences, are they not?"

He turned to her. "May I lay some facts before you, my lady?"

"Certainly," she answered and her outward

calmness belied the uncertainty in her heart at that moment.

"You will forgive my frankness?"

"Yes, Lieutenant Stacey."

"You have been married, I believe, only three weeks, yet little more than that the earl was paying court quite publicly to a very beautiful lady by the name of Caroline Kingsley. Not only is she beautiful but she is also very rich, and it is well-known the Glenbrookes, due to successive generations of free-spenders, needs must marry rich wives. It is firmly believed that Glenbrooke is being dunned by his creditors."

"I did not know that," Lucinda said in some dismay.

"Depend upon it, it is true." The lieutenant smiled grimly. "To continue; it was expected that their betrothal would be announced within the week, for Glenbrooke was dangling after this beauty for most of the Season and his intent was not in doubt. But to everyone's surprise—not the least to the earl's, it is said—her betrothal was announced to the Duke of Derwent."

"Is it not possible," asked Lucinda in some bewilderment, "that he decided upon my hand rather than Miss Kingsley's at the very last moment? We met but a short time before our wedding."

He smiled at her. "Let me assure you, Lady Glenbrooke, when it comes to beauty, there can be no comparison between the two." His smile faded.

"But why, if he were intending to marry you in what could only be a matter of days, would he offer for another?"

Lucinda put her hands up to her cheeks. "Perhaps then he fell in love with me afterwards."

"But so soon, Lady Glenbrooke. Within days? Broken hearts are not mended so soon. It is quite some feat even for a man of such ability and ingenuity as Glenbrooke. However, I fear you have not heard the worst."

She looked up sharply. "The worst, Lieutenant Stacey?"

He swallowed hard. "I admit this week Glenbrooke's casual attitude to his new bride both puzzled and angered me, especially as I knew about his partiality to Miss Kingsley, not to mention another . . . lady whose name I would not mention in the same room as that in which you sit. Now, I learn from the friends with whom I am staying that some years ago Mr Courtney-Smythe, for whom I have the greatest regard, imposed a condition on the earl; a condition of inheritance." Lucinda watched him carefully. "The condition stipulates that the earl, to inherit the fortune and receive a handsome wedding gift in addition, must be married by the time he is thirty, and his birthday, I believe, is very soon."

She stared at him in astonishment for a moment or two before asking in a hushed voice, "How do your hosts know of this?"

"Because the countess, with whom they are usually intimate, has bemoaned the fact many times during her visits." She said nothing and he added, "It is not just one of these facts that trouble me, Lady Glenbrooke, but all of them together. Even the odd occurrence of an accident so soon after the marriage."

Lucinda looked up then. "What has my accident to do with anything? Glenbrooke's curricle collided with the stage and I fell from it and knocked my head." She shook her head as if to clear it of the miscellany of disturbing facts he had told her. "Perhaps the earl was in love with Miss Kingsley and only asked me to be his wife so that he could become Great Uncle Percival's beneficiary. Perhaps also I agreed to marry him only because I wanted a good name and a position in Society. I cannot conceive what my accident could have to do with such an arrangement, save it being extremely ill-timed."

The lieutenant rubbed his hands across his lips. "I wish I knew, Lady Glenbrooke, but I am most concerned for you. It is extremely unlikely that any man with an ounce of propriety would convey his bride in a racing curricle."

She swallowed hard. "I think I should have enjoyed it, Lieutenant Stacey. I may have pressed Glenbrooke into bringing me here in such a manner. In fact I am sure of it."

"Unfortunately you can only surmise; you cannot *know*." He snatched up her hand quickly and before the startled girl could draw it away he had pressed it to his lips. "My dearest countess, I have known Glenbrooke and his set for a good many years, and believe me when I say there is something decidedly fishy about the situation here."

Lucinda withdrew her hand. Her cheeks had taken on an even rosier hue. "That is a ridiculous suggestion, Lieutenant Stacey, and one that I hope I may never hear you voice again."

"I do beg your pardon, Lady Glenbrooke," he said in some distress. "I cannot bear your anger. Please say you forgive me. I shall not know a moment's peace until you do."

"Of course," she answered, moved by his obvious distress.

Her heart was beating fast, her thoughts confused. She was troubled by what she had been told and in addition were her own, unsubstantiated, misgiving which she dared not voice. In truth she did not want to believe Dareth guilty of some treachery, but it seemed she had been used by him in order that he should be made Great Uncle Percival's beneficiary and receive part of his inheritance in the form of a wedding gift; something of which he was so badly in need.

Lucinda and Lieutenant Stacey were staring at each other, their individual thoughts a jumble, when the door opened and none other than the earl came in. He stopped abruptly when he caught sight of the two occupants of the room. Both Lucinda and the lieutenant jumped to their feet, both, to the earl's eyes, wearing guilty expressions on their faces.

He looked slowly from one to the other and when, a moment later, he had recovered from his surprise he smiled urbanely at Lucinda and, coming into the room, said, "Fencham was quite right when he said he fancied you'd come in here. But," he added, a mite more severely, "he was wrong in thinking you were alone."

"I came across to ask the countess if she would do me the honour of riding with me this morning," muttered the lieutenant.

"I am not allowed to ride," Lucinda explained quickly, glad of something to say. "Dr Bishop believes my injury might result in occasional bouts of faintness, so it would not be wise for me to ride just at the moment."

The lieutenant nodded and, casting a glance at the earl who showed no disposition to leave the room again, said in grudging tones, "You will, no doubt, wish to be private with your wife."

"Indeed, I had hoped so, Stacey," he answered heartily. "There has been such an influx of visitors and a preponderance of work for me to attend to, I have hardly seen Lucy since she rose from her sickbed."

"I shall take my leave of you," the lieutenant answered stiffly and then, taking Lucinda's hand briefly added, "If I may, I shall call upon you again, Lady Glenbrooke."

"Yes, you will be most welcome," she answered

quickly, glancing hesitantly at Dareth and inject-
ing warmth into her voice in an effort to make
amends for the earl's churlishness, "and any time
you choose to call."

The lieutenant bowed stiffly to them both and
when Lucinda hurried over to the window with
him, he stopped just outside and said in a low,
harsh voice, "I need not reiterate my feelings for
you, Lady Glenbrooke. You know well that I am
your devoted servant and always shall be. If you
ever find yourself in need of a friend, please do
not hesitate to come to me."

Before she could answer, he had turned and was
hurrying off as fast as his lame leg would allow.
Lucinda stared after him and a moment or two
later when she roused herself to return to the sitting room, she turned to find she was face to face
with the earl. Starting guiltily she suspected he
had overheard all the lieutenant had said and wondered what construction he would put on his
words.

"Did you want me for something?" she asked in
a bright voice as she brushed past him to go back
into the house. She was unusually unnerved, both
by his presence and by what Lieutenant Stacey
had told her.

He followed her back into the room. "Would
you like to go riding with me?"

She whirled round to face him. The jumbled
thoughts were still coursing through her brain,
making no coherent pattern in her mind.

"But I thought. . . . Didn't you just say. . . ?"

Impatiently he waved away the excuse his mother had used to prevent Lucinda discovering she could not ride, something which every young lady of any breeding learned to do at a very early age.

"There can be no harm in your sitting up with me. If you feel faint you will be in no danger of falling off. I shall," he added with a grimness Lucinda did not notice, "hold you tightly."

She flushed with pleasure at the prospect, forgetting the preceding exchange with the lieutenant almost immediately. She did not want to remember it whilst there was an ounce of a possibility it was not true.

"I should like that above all things!" she answered excitedly. "I believe there is a riding habit amongst the clothes Fraser has altered for me."

At such obvious pleasure being evident on her face, the earl was once more assailed with remorse. He too had almost forgotten the irritation Lieutenant Stacey's unexpected presence had caused him.

He smiled slightly. "I shall have one of my horses made ready and brought round while you change."

Lucinda nodded eagerly before lifting her skirt free of her ankles and rushing from the room as if she were afraid he would change his mind.

However, as she left the room his smile immediately faded. He wondered what Digby Stacey had been saying to Lucinda with such intensity when he had come upon them. It seemed his mother might well be right in her supposition that an attachment was being formed between the two, if their red and guilty faces were anything by which to judge. The thought gave the earl no pleasure, and, turning angrily on his heel, he marched out of the room.

Chapter Nine

With the sun and the wind in her face, Lucinda felt glorious. She felt carefree and unbelievably happy.

She had not imagined riding such an enjoyable occupation, and had to admit to herself that if one was unfortunate enough to lose one's memory, at least enjoying every pursuit as if for the first time was in some way a recompense.

They were well out into the country now and ahead of them loomed the sinister old stones of what was once the abbey. Outlined against a blue and white sky they looked forlorn and yet majestic. As they approached, the chestnut mare slowed its pace and Lucinda felt as breathless as if she, herself, had been galloping down the shady lanes.

The mare cantered to a stop and the earl slid to the ground, lightly lifting her down too.

"I did enjoy my ride!" she exclaimed, putting two hands up to her flushed cheeks. She glanced around her quickly, "So this is where it all started."

He let the reins go and the mare wandered off. He glanced around him too. "As you can see there is very little here of interest any more."

Lucinda gazed around her too, her eyes passing over the broken stones which lay about them, marking what was once the outer perimiter of the abbey. One small wall was still intact, but all the stones were overgrown with moss and weeds, and wild flowers struggled to the sunlight from every nook and cranny.

"It has atmosphere," she said after a moment or two, and then twirling round, exclaimed, "Oh, I do love the countryside! I love everything about it, Dareth. I may have lived at Hampstead, but the Heath cannot be such glorious countryside as this. I feel as if I've never been out of the city before."

The earl watched her carefully and then turned away and went to sit on the low wall, facing the fields beyond the abbey. Lucinda felt confused. She went up to him and he looked up at her when she reached his side.

"Melissa's riding habit becomes you very well. Far more, in fact, than it ever suited her."

The dark green velvet was, indeed, becoming as Lucinda was well aware, but nevertheless her cheeks became pink. His compliments always pleased her but in this one she sensed more seriousness than she had noted before.

She was toying with the riding whip he had allowed her to carry since they set out. "Has my trunk been found yet?"

"No trunk has been found," he answered quite truthfully, thinking how tiresome this whole business was becoming. He longed to tell her the truth, but perversely dreaded doing so now.

"You may choose a wardrobe of clothes when you return to London," he said, still not looking at her.

"London," she echoed and he sensed the excitement in her voice.

He glanced at her then and away again. "My mother will help you choose a new wardrobe."

"Melissa's clothes are quite lovely and will suffice for some considerable time. I beg you, Dareth, don't go to any expense on my account when it is far from necessary." He smiled slightly and she added, a little mournfully, "I feel as if I could spend the rest of my days here quite cheerfully. . . ."

"Lucy. . . ." he began, in a gentle voice. Now was the time, and be damned with all else! he thought.

But she went on, her eyes filling involuntarily with tears. "Oh yes, I know it will be better for me to be in London where sights and people are familiar to me. Besides, you must be growing tired of rusticating."

"Have you no recollections yet?"

She shook her head. When he said nothing more

she glanced back at the overgrown remains of the abbey, and then sat down beside him on the wall. "The ruin is depressing," she said thoughtfully. "I like it much better when we face this way."

He laughed at that, and she said, still serious, "Buildings are nothing when there are no people in them to give them life, especially on a day like this."

She sighed and he said, "What a strange girl you are."

She looked at him. "Do I seem strange to you, Dareth?"

"Let us say, I have got to know you better during this past week."

"But we have hardly spoken to each other alone this week."

"That does not mean I haven't noticed you, or attended everything you have said with interest." As she glanced downwards in confusion he ran his finger along her nose. "You have quite an assortment of freckles there."

Automatically she too touched her nose. "I know. Your mother was very upset and Fraser spent quite an hour, first trying to remove them with lemon juice and then, when that failed, she tried to hide them. She was not successful I'm afraid."

"That was fortunate. I happen to like your freckles."

She looked at him for a long moment and then

said very quickly, "Great Uncle Percival will be leaving soon, Dareth."

She looked at him hopefully but he simply said, "He has grown very fond of you."

"And I of him. I shall miss him excessively." She glanced up at him again. "May I visit with him in Bath?"

The earl looked taken aback for a moment or two before replying with equanimity, "I imagine he will insist upon it."

"I worry about him, Dareth." The earl was surprised once more. Lucinda was playing with the riding whip. "He is old, is he not?"

"He has reached quite an advanced age."

She looked at him appealingly. "I don't believe he is too well, Dareth. He looked very drawn last night."

"I have never seen Great Uncle Percival in anything other than the best of health. I only hope I may reach his age in such good repair."

Lucinda nodded and smiled weakly. "Perhaps you are right, and I am fretting unnecessarily. You have known him for so much longer than I." She glanced across at the field in front of them, which came up almost to the ruined abbey. In it a few dozen sheep gambolled happily in the morning sunshine.

"The lambs are quite delightful," she said brightly, sensing in the earl a strange mood. There were so many unaccountable silences between them. "May I go closer?"

"Yes, of course you may."

She jumped up and ran across the narrow strip of pasture, aware that his eyes were upon her all the time. She wondered why he was suddenly so thoughtful, why she was so suddenly ill at ease, and why the prospect of returning to Glenbrooke Abbey with his arms about her was so alarming.

So great was her confusion she didn't hear him approach and she started violently when he came up to her. He appeared not to notice her consternation; it was possible that he did not, for he was looking at the sheep too.

"Which one do you like best?" he asked.

Diverted, Lucinda replied, pointing into the field, "That one over there. I've been watching him for an age and he's so frisky. Much livelier than any of the others. Just look at him, Dareth!"

"Wait where you are for just one moment," he told her as he opened the gate.

She watched in some bewilderment for a moment or two and then laughed delightedly as he scooped up the object of her interest and carried it back to her.

"His mother is following you," she cried.

"She can have her offspring back in a moment or two," he told Lucinda as she stroked the lamb's soft wool.

"He's so sweet," she murmured.

"He is a she."

Lucinda laughed again as the ewe hovered anxiously around. "I might have known. Only a female could display so much delight in such a lovely day. A male would have taken it all for granted."

The amusement had gone from his eyes. He was looking at her in a strange way that caused her to feel confused again.

"Do you have a ribbon in your hair?"

At the unexpectedness of such a question Lucinda's eyes grew large. "Why, yes. Yes, I do. Why do you ask?"

"I ask because I want it."

Hesitating only a moment she untied her hat and removing it, handed him the ribbon from her hair.

"Take our little friend," he invited.

She hesitated yet again, still puzzled. "I may drop her."

"I doubt it."

He bundled the lamb into her arms and Lucinda rubbed her face against its wool. "I wish I could keep her. She's so adorable."

The earl fastened the ribbon around the lamb's neck. "It would be cruel to separate her from her mother at so tender an age, but with this ribbon around her neck you will have no difficulty in recognising her immediately each time you come to see her."

"What a beautiful thought." Her eyes were shining. She handed the lamb back into his arms. "I feel as if she belongs to me now. I shall watch her progress with all the pride of a mother."

He set the lamb free and it skipped away, the blue ribbon proudly displayed around its neck. Lucinda laughed delightedly. "There isn't a smarter animal on the whole estate."

When she looked back at him he was gazing at her and she had to look away again.

"Lucy," he said abruptly, "there is something I must tell you."

Some of the light went out of her eyes. "Is it about our . . . relationship?"

It was his turn to look away. "Yes," he answered heavily. "There is something I want you to know. . . ."

"Then please tell me, Dareth. You needn't fear to speak freely to me."

She had rested both hands on the fence and was staring into the distance. She found she was gripping the fence very tightly indeed. When, after a moment, he was still silent she looked up again. "You want to tell me you don't love me," she said.

He seemed incapable of speech and her heart sank to its lowest depth as he turned away from her. And then he said in a very bemused voice she could hardly hear, "That isn't quite true. I do love you, Lucy. Very much indeed."

For one very long moment she said nothing and then when the true realisation of his words came to her, she flung her arms around his neck. The earl was momentarily astonished but then his arms tightened round her too.

"I was so afraid you didn't. I thought you

were going to say something quite different."

He held her away and searched her face for a moment or two before kissing her gently on the lips.

"I have waited all week for you to do that," she said breathlessly.

His arms tightened around her again. Lucinda was no longer shy or worried. She responded eagerly to the kisses he bestowed upon her lips, cheeks and neck, as they stood with no regard for time, imprisoned in each other arms.

At last, still closely locked in his embrace, she said, "How strange life is."

"Very strange," he agreed.

"I have no memory of anything and yet I know instinctively that I love you. Nothing else matters, does it, Dareth?"

She pulled away so that she could look at him. His smile was a little strained as he answered, "Nothing else matters, Lucy."

He drew her close again and she laid her head against his shoulder as he caressed her hair. "We needn't be apart any longer," she said, sighing contentedly.

He held her away again and she looked at him questioningly. He seemed to be staring at her for an age. "There are some matters I must attend to first, Lucy," he said, as if he had just remembered something.

"What matters?"

"I can't tell you just yet, but soon everything

will be clear, so trust me a while longer, will you?"

His hand gently cupped her cheek. She nodded slowly, but there was still a question in her eyes. He drew her to him and kissed her again. Nothing mattered to her then. He let her go and whistled for the mare which came trotting up to them.

"Must we go just yet?" she asked in dismay. "It's so lovely out here."

He smiled down at her and there was no mistaking the fondness she saw in his eyes. "We shall come here as often as you wish, but just at this moment I am anxious to have words with Great Uncle Percival before he leaves."

Lucinda turned away to hide her dismay. There was something troubling him still and she feared what it might be, despite his reassurances. He stooped down and retrieved her hat and the riding crop. Both had slipped from her fingers a long time ago.

As he handed them to her she gave him a reassuring smile and put her hands to her hair which had become somewhat disarranged. "I must look quite disordered."

He gazed at her gravely for a moment or two, brushing a stray strand of hair from her cheek. "You look delightful," he said at last as her cheeks flooded with colour. He put his hands around her waist to lift her up in to the saddle and as he did so he kissed her again.

"I shall always remember this morning as something very special in my life," she said. "It's like a new beginning."

"It is for me too, Lucy; more so than you could ever imagine."

So saying he lifted her and a moment later was sitting up behind her. His grip tightened as he took the reins and Lucinda snuggled back into his arms.

"I am so glad I am not allowed to ride on my own," she murmured.

"You will change your mind when the hunting season is upon us," he answered wryly, bestowing a kiss on her cool cheek.

She turned slightly to give him a wicked look. "There is lots of lovely time before that."

But his only answer was to spur the mare into a gallop and no more could be said.

When he helped Lucinda down from the mare, the earl kept one of her hands tightly imprisoned in his. She smiled up at him as he raised it to his lips momentarily. The past hour had made the world of difference to her happiness. No longer was she uncertain of him, or her own feelings.

As she smoothed the skirt of her riding habit she asked, "Do I look presentable?"

"You always do. You need no gilding, my love."

Together they walked hand in hand into the great hall. For the first time Lucinda felt she was actually a part of it. For the first time she knew she was entitled to belong, and she drew a sigh of deep satisfaction.

As they entered the hall she stopped and looked at him seriously. "Until now I could never imagine myself as your wife, Dareth."

The earl found, at that moment, anything he might say was stuck in his throat, but he was saved the embarrassment by his mother's familiar voice, saying, "Dareth! Thank goodness you have come!"

She was hurrying down the stairs, evidently suffering some distress. The earl and Lucinda exchanged worried looks and, dropping her hand, he hurried over to greet his mother who was far too upset to have noticed the sudden intimacy between the two.

"Mother, why are you in such a taking?"

"Uncle Percival," she gasped, biting back a sob.

The earl stiffened and Lucinda hurried forward. "What is it?" she asked, looking from one to the other in alarm. "What has happened to put her in such a pucker?"

The countess took a deep breath and was helped to a seat by the young couple. She looked up at the anxious face of her son. "He has been taken mortally ill, Dareth."

Lucinda gasped in alarm and the earl drew away sharply. "Be precise, Mother."

She swallowed loudly and Lucinda handed her a handkerchief which the countess pressed to her lips. "Please try to be calm," urged the girl, "and tell us what has happened to poor Great Uncle Percival."

The countess sank back into the chair and the earl said to Lucinda, "She is never rational in a crisis."

"Then it is well that I am."

The earl stared at her in surprise and then hurriedly transferred his attention back to his mother. "Well, Mother? How is he?"

"Very bad according to Dr Bishop. He is with him now and does not expect him to last the night."

Lucinda gave a little cry of alarm and the earl attempted to give her a reassuring smile while attending to his mother.

"He just crumpled, Dareth. It was so awful to see. But we got him to his bed and Dr Bishop came just as fast as he could. I have never seen anyone look quite so dreadful."

The earl, having recovered from his shock, became thoughtful. "It is most unfortunate for it to have happened just now, while he is here."

Lucinda was looking at him and there was a question in her eyes, but he avoided meeting them. The fact that she trusted him so implicitly was a sweet torment.

The countess groped for his hand. "Dareth, he has asked for a lawyer to be fetched. Bracknell, after summoning Dr Bishop, remained in Leicester to locate one."

The earl could say nothing. He continued to stare at his mother until Lucinda said hurriedly, with a perceptiveness not really appreciated by the other two, "I shall go and fetch your vinaigrette, Lady Glenbrooke."

The countess looked at the girl as if she had only just seen her, and then she started violently. "Yes, yes, my dear, do so, if you please."

They both watched the demure figure as she went upstairs, hurrying, although so graceful she did not seem to do so. When she had reached the top without looking back, the countess drew her son down beside her.

"I wonder what his purpose is in sending for a lawyer?" mused the earl.

"Is it not obvious?" answered his mother in a hushed tone. "Ill Uncle Percival may be, but he was still able to talk and in full command of his faculties." The earl gave his mother his undivided attention now that Lucinda had gone. "He said he'd not expected you to marry so he'd written his will accordingly years ago. Now that he's been given notice to quit he wants to put the matter to rights. Said he'd intended to do it when he returned to Bath." She wrung her hands in anguish. "Foolish, foolish man. It is quite plain he has only just now made you his beneficiary."

"I must stop him," said the earl, starting towards the stairs.

His mother caught his arm and pulled him down to her side again. "You cannot do that, not while he is so ill. It will be the end of him to learn of this ... mistake now. The lawyer may yet not arrive in time, and no harm will have been done. If you are named as his beneficiary because of your marriage you will have Lucinda to thank for it, so we shall use the money to benefit her. Uncle Percival would be perfectly happy about that."

The earl drew in a sharp breath. "If there is no alternative, we shall certainly do that."

He got to his feet as Lucinda came back down the stairs with the countess's vinaigrette. Before she was halfway down, the doctor appeared at the top.

"Is there any change?" asked the earl immediately.

The doctor shook his head, his long face more mournful than ever. "We can expect none, my lord. Mr Courtney-Smythe has a stout constitution but the seizure was too much for him. The end may come at any time." Lucinda's eyes filled with tears again and the sight of her distress tugged at the earl's heart. He had never thought to be moved by a woman and the sensation was more satisfactory than he would have imagined.

The doctor added, after clearing his throat, "The patient has been asking for the young countess. I would advise her to hurry."

Lucinda turned to go back up the stairs. "I shall come immediately."

"Do remember," warned the countess, "that the child has not long been out of her sickbed herself."

Lucinda smiled sadly. "Have no fear on my account, my lady. I would very much like to bear dear Great Uncle Percival company in his time of pain. My only regret is that I am unable to do more than that."

She handed the countess her vinaigrette and hurried back to where the doctor was waiting to escort her to his patient.

"Young countess, indeed," scoffed the earl's mother. "Who could have imagined the chit would do so well in the role? I believe she has bewitched the old man."

He drew her closer to him. "Mother, I believe she has bewitched us all."

Chapter Ten

Percival Courtney-Smythe did not, in fact, die that night, nor on any of ten successive nights that he lay desperately ill, and by the time a fortnight had passed, Dr Bishop pronounced him out of danger.

During those anxious two weeks, Lucinda was with the invalid at every moment she was not either sleeping or eating. The earl saw her only at meal times and on occasions for a few moments when they had little time or inclination for anything other than the briefest exchange.

Although disappointed that he saw so little of her, the earl was in one way glad. Most certainly he wanted to hold her in his arms again but he bowed to the wisdom of waiting until such time that all barriers of restraint could be broken down between them and they could start their association afresh. Of course, he did realize that because he had declared himself whilst matters were in such a tangle, it meant that they could not begin again entirely afresh, but with a wholly uncharacteristic naivete he assumed their love would weather all storms.

The improvement in Percival Courtney-Smythe's health continued well into the third week. It was then that the earl came upon Lucinda quite unexpectedly early one fine afternoon as he returned to the house from the stables where he had been inspecting his horses. He was not at all pleased to see her in conversation with Lieutenant Stacey who had called in on several occasions during the past few weeks. Ostensibly it was to have news of the invalid, but the earl was not so easily fooled; Lieutenant Stacey had come to have sight of Lucinda. To the earl's gratification, on those occasions, Lucinda had been too busy to see him.

At the sound of his footsteps on the path, Lucinda turned and smiled with pleasure at seeing him. Although his demeanour unbent at the sight of so sunny a person, he did not return her smile, realising in some dismay that the emotion he always experienced when he saw the two together was in fact jealousy.

But in view of the smile on her face he too managed to force one to his lips as he came closer, for not to do so would have been churlish.

"Dearest, Lieutenant Stacey has been kind enough to call in and enquire after Great Uncle Percival."

The earl and the lieutenant acknowledged each other with stiff bows. "It is indeed a kind thought, lieutenant. No doubt my . . . Lucy has told you our invalid is making splendid progress."

"I was delighted to hear it," murmured the other, but his displeasure at having his tête-à-tête with Lucinda interrupted was evident.

"You are still with the Northboroughs at Lansdown Manor, are you not? I should have thought such prolonged rustication boring to you."

The lieutenant's manner was equally as strained. "Usually it is, Glenbrooke, but for some reason," he continued to look at Lucinda, "not on this occasion. Of course I shall remove to Brighton with Gerald Northborough in about a month's time." He looked once more at Lucinda. "Again let me say how delighted I am to hear that the old gentleman is much improved, Lady Glenbrooke. If rumours are to be believed, it is your hand which snatched him back from death."

She laughed delightedly. "Such rumours are vastly exaggerated."

"I think not," said the earl, studying her carefully. "Lucy has hardly had a moment to herself since Mr Courtney-Smythe was stricken. She is pale beyond belief, although she would not for the world admit her exhaustion."

Lucinda dimpled at his concern and the lieutenant said, "Yes, indeed. I, most certainly agree with you there, Glenbrooke. The countess must rest. I shall take my leave of you immediately in order that you may do so, Lady Glenbrooke."

She began to protest, but the earl said, "I insist, Lucy. Great Uncle Percival cannot need you so desperately now."

"Very well. I shall go to my room presently. I have managed to persuade Great Uncle Percival to sit near the terrace with the window slightly open, for a while at least. I have persuaded him a little fresh air in moderation is not at all harmful. He is already well enough to speak of leaving by the end of the week, although I have warned him of the inadvisability of such a course."

She laid one hand on the earl's arm. "He was asking after you only this morning and would, I am sure, be pleased if you were to bear him company for a while."

"If it will mean you can rest, I shall do so most willingly."

"That is kind of you, dear." She looked at the lieutenant. "And I shall walk with you to your carriage, Lieutenant Stacey."

The man beamed at the prospect and the earl, who could think of no way of stopping them, took his leave and went to find his great uncle. He was more than ever determined to end the charade.

It was some considerable time later when the earl, still laughing, emerged from the sitting room. The first person upon whom he set eyes was his mother, and apparently in one of her states of crisis.

"Dareth, oh, Dareth, of all things!" she cried, bearing down on him the moment he emerged from his meeting with his great uncle. "As if everything that has happened this month isn't outside of enough, I have just received this letter."

She waved the document under his nose. The earl was still laughing but he collected himself sufficiently to examine and then recognise the seal it bore.

"Isn't that Sir Richard Crosbie's seal?" he asked in surprise. "Is *he* about to visit us too? I declare apart from Mrs Cartwright his is the only presence we have lacked these past four weeks."

"If only that were all, Dareth. You will hardly credit what has happened. Only fancy, Dareth! Dickie has offered for me!"

At this news the earl began to laugh anew. "I thought at the very least we had received startling news."

The countess relaxed a little and was able to smile too. "How can you remain so calm? It was so unexpected."

"It was not totally unexpected to me, and if *you* can say so after more than thirty years of his admiration and constant company, you are not the woman I have always believed you to be."

She clutched at his arm. "What am I to answer? The poor creature declares he hasn't the courage to ask me to my face."

"I'm not entirely surprised at that either. After all these years of bachelorhood, he must be still half hoping you'll refuse."

"And shall I?"

"My dearest Mama, it can be your decision and your decision alone."

"I was very happy with your father, Dareth," she said dreamily. "When Henry offered for me there was no question of my acceptance, despite it being Dickie who was first on the scene. But I am far too young to remain a dowager all my life, even if I am to be a grandmother. My children no longer need me. And Dickie *is* a dear."

"You have your answer, I believe."

She smiled dreamily again. "Yes, I believe I have." She looked at him. "Do you really not mind, dearest? You won't think I am being disloyal to your father?"

"You were, to him, the perfect wife for more than thirty years, Mother, and that was in no small measure due to your being contented. I am sure he wouldn't want you to cease being contented now, which you will be if you remain a widow with nothing but a clutch of grandchildren to occupy your time, for depend upon it, Melissa will produce a clutch. Your future still lies in a full social life."

"You are a dear," she said happily. "I couldn't accept his offer if you didn't approve."

"I have always had the highest regard for Sir

Richard," her son answered, adding drily, "and never more than now."

"And it is a fact, you will not want me even in the Dower House once you have a bride."

The earl waved one languid hand in the air. "Oh, as to that, Lucy loves you."

She chuckled. "I am not funning."

He was eyeing her coldly now. "Neither am I."

Her laughter faded. "You are earnest over the girl?"

"Very much so."

The countess looked stunned but managed to say, "I should have known this would happen. It is merely justice."

"Do you mind, Mother?" he asked in a more gentle voice.

She shook her head dumbly. "I have to admit a fondness for the chit. But I fear it bodes ill, Dareth."

He stiffened. "What do you mean?"

She drew herself up. "I have never seen another woman who consistently beats her husband at both billiards and at card games. I don't know how your pride can bear it. I tell you that girl is storing trouble for the time your eyes are no longer filled with moonshine."

He laughed out loud again and kissed her forehead as she said, "My word, if we take into account Melissa's baby, this is going to be the most hectic of years." She drew away from him. "And this means no one will have to know of my mistake."

"Great Uncle Percival already knows."

"Oh, you cannot have told him, Dareth. You promised! If you intend to marry Lucinda after all, there surely was no need."

"I'm sorry, Mother, but I had to tell him the whole story. I refuse to approach Lucy with all this pretence between us. The truth must be known to all of those involved, including Great Uncle Percival."

"You are, as usual, right," said the countess, her tone more subdued than usual. "Is he terribly angry?"

"On the contrary, he is exceedingly amused by the whole episode. He appreciates that there was no real intent to defraud him. We are fortunate indeed he has taken such an attitude. It would have been excessively uncomfortable if he had not. Of course, Great Uncle Percival does have the advantage of knowing you even better than I do. He is delighted, of course, that I mean to marry Lucy, and for the right reasons."

"And Lucinda? Has she been told yet?"

The earl's own face became taut. "I must go and tell her now. I cannot remain silent any longer. You do understand that, Mother, don't you?"

The countess nodded her agreement. "I shall be glad when there is nothing more to be hidden. We can start afresh."

"I hope you may be right."

Her eyes grew wide again. "Pray tell me why I may *not* be right? Do you think it feasible that she would refuse to become your wife? The girl has a fondness for you. How can it be otherwise?"

He smiled again, but grimly. "She has a fondness for me now, but that is not to say she will still feel the same after I have spoken to her."

"Faugh! Love is not so easily destroyed."

"Again I say, I hope you may be right."

Abruptly he moved across the hall and, startled, the countess hurried after him. "Where are you going?"

"To see Lucy, right now. I'm not waiting another moment."

"But she is alone, in her rooms."

He stopped and laughed harshly. "I have already compromised her, Mother, on several occasions. Once more will make no odds."

She caught his arm. "Dareth, one more word before you go. What did Uncle Percival say about the *will?*"

"Oh, the will," answered her son as if he had only just remembered it, as indeed he had; Lucinda bore far more heavily on his mind. He leaned against the bannister indolently. "Great Uncle Percival told me about his new will. Apparently when he made the old one, he could not find it in him to be hard-hearted enough to cut me off completely whether I was married by the time I reached thirty or not. The will he made seven years ago made me the main beneficiary in any event."

The countess sank down on to the bottom step, her shawl falling from her shoulders. "So he was hoaxing us all the time."

"Yes," he snapped. "Amusing, is it not?"

"Very," his mother answered with equal grimness. Then looking up at him, she asked, frowning slightly, "But what was the meaning of his sending for a lawyer the day he took ill, if you were already to receive his estate?"

The earl gave a short, sharp laugh. "Didn't I tell you he was no fool, Mother? To use his own words, he thought there was something 'havey-cavey' about my 'marriage' which was so secret and so convenient, especially as Lucy was able to tell him nothing about herself. So, to safeguard her, he made her his beneficiary instead."

The countess gave a shriek and before she could recover herself, he had turned on his heel and was already at the top of the stairs. She fell back against the wall, almost paralysed with shock, and then, after a moment or two, she began to laugh too. She laughed so hard at the irony of it all she thought she might burst.

Lucinda was sitting at her window seat, gazing out at the parkland which stretched as far as the eye could see. She never tired of the view, nor did she tire of wandering about the grounds, ever discovering something she had never seen before.

Far from feeling tired, she felt revitalised at having something useful to do these past weeks so coming to her room, ostensibly to rest, was only done to please the earl. She would have been happier by far remaining downstairs with him. When there came a knock on the door she turned eagerly to bid her visitor enter. When she saw it was the earl, she was momentarily startled, and then more than delighted to see him.

A smile of welcome transformed her face but no such smile was reflected on his face. He looked ill at ease and to Lucinda it seemed a long time ago since he had held her in his arms and kissed her with a tenderness that sent her blood racing through her veins. Her pulses quickened just at the sight of him coming into the room. The past month had changed her considerably, she realised now, but in some ways she was still as uncertain as she had been then.

"Do I disturb you?" he asked, coming hesitantly into the room.

"I would rather have your company than remain alone," she answered in all truth.

At that he allowed himself a small smile. He crossed the room and, sitting down to face her, he took her hand and raised it briefly to his lips. He thought he had never seen her look so lovely. In her pale yellow muslin gown with its demure neckline and short puffed sleeves, her skin so pale it appeared transparent, she looked almost too ethereal to be real.

After she had borne his contemplation for a moment or two, she asked, "Have you been keeping company with Great Uncle Percival?"

"Yes," came his heavy answer. "He and I have had a serious discussion, which because of his illness I was forced to postpone until now. Lucy ... there is something I have to tell you, and it is rather difficult to explain."

She raised her eyes and searched his face anxiously before asking, "Do you wish to confess that our marriage was one of convenience so you would be married in time to be made Great Uncle Percival's heir and receive his wedding gift?"

He stared at her in blank astonishment and then she said, her face softening a little, "Lieutenant Stacey told me weeks ago." He started, but she pressed her hand onto his. "No, do not be angry with him, dearest. You would have acted in exactly the same manner if the positions were changed."

"He did not speak from a desire to protect you, Lucy, but from a wish to cause mischief to me, I fear. Why on earth didn't you mention it earlier?"

She smiled. "Because it is of no matter. He told me also of your partiality for Miss Kingsley, but that does not matter either." He looked out of the window and was able only to nod briefly. "We have found each other here, Dareth," she went on in a gentle voice that threatened to tear him to pieces. "What went before hardly matters now."

"Damn it, it does!" swore the earl, thumping

his fist down on the ledge of the window. A bird that had been singing merrily in the chestnut tree outside the window rose up in great alarm with a frantic beating of its wings.

"What he has told you is the least of it."

Lucinda's eyes opened wide. "Is there more? I refuse to believe Lieutenant Stacey's other assumption that, having married me, you attempted to throw me from your curricle."

He gave a broken little laugh and, passing his hand wearily across his face, said in a voice shaking with emotion, "I have never had such a difficult task to perform, Lucy, and your good-natured acceptance of all this does not make it easier."

She leaned forward slightly. "You are alarming me, Dareth. Pray tell me what remains of the story, without any further delay."

He still could not look at her. He longed to take her in his arms and soothe away her fear and the hurt she would soon come to feel, but he knew he could not trust himself to touch her.

"We are *not* married," he said in a low voice.

A moment of incredible silence elapsed before Lucinda cried out, "*Not* married! But everyone calls me Lady Glenbrooke. I do not understand!"

He said nothing; he just continued to stare out of the window, seeing nothing but the bewilderment on her face.

"Do not tell me I am your. . . ."

"No, no," he said quickly, turning back to her then. He took her hand and cradled it to his cheek. "I had never seen you before the day you had the accident and were brought here. Let me explain, and it can be over with once and for all."

She withdrew her hand and lowered her eyes. "Please do so," she said and her voice was uneven.

She remained head bowed and motionless as he explained as fully as he could everything that had happened from her fall from the stagecoach to this morning when Great Uncle Percival had told him he had made Lucinda his heiress. Even this elicited no response from her.

When he had finished the sad tale and fell silent, looking at her anxiously for her reaction, she looked up at him at last and he hated to see the pain in her eyes.

"So I am not the Countess of Glenbrooke, but a penniless orphan who was about to go into service. There could hardly be a larger difference. There is no aunt in Hampstead, no impetuous romance. There is nothing at all. I am nothing at all. And yet, I am not surprised. Inside me all this time I have been aware of a strangeness of everything I have seen and done. All the time I knew I was not worthy of you."

"You're most worthy," he said in heartfelt tones, watching her agony helplessly.

She appeared not to hear him. She gave a little broken laugh. "A penniless orphan. I feel more like the Countess of Glenbrooke."

"You are no longer penniless, Lucy. . . ."

"Why has he willed me this money? And the

wedding gift. Did he know I was not your wife? If I were, surely the inheritance would be yours anyway."

The earl sighed heavily. "Quite so, but Great Uncle Percival was simply safeguarding you by making you the beneficiary instead of me. As matters stand he was wise to do so."

He reached over to take her hand but as he did so she jumped to her feet and ran across the room. She gripped on to one of the bedposts, clinging on to it for support.

"My accident was a timely one. My loss of memory even more so. Great Uncle Percival obviously did not stipulate what kind of a wife you must have. Any one would do, even an orphan. I was sufficient to defraud an old man."

"I have explained," said the earl in some distress, "no attempt to defraud was made. It was all quite innocently started. My mother has always been impulsive, and before we knew it the servants were congratulating me, and it went on from there. My great uncle finds the whole episode quite amusing."

"Well, I can't," she said in a strangled voice. "But then, I am not gentry, am I? The countess must have found my airs and graces very amusing too."

"You have no airs and graces, my dear, and if you believe ill of my mother, then you cannot know her well. Madcap she may be, but wicked she certainly is not. When she realised the results to you she was most distressed."

"All the lies and pretence, all these weeks. I can hardly bear to think of it."

He came up to her then and placed his hands gently on her shoulders. "Then don't think about it, Lucy. It's all to be forgotten. No one but the few of us will ever know of this unintentional muddle."

She gave a harsh laugh. "Acknowledging me as your wife for a whole month cannot be regarded as unintentional."

"It will," he said softly in her ear, "be a fact as soon as it can be arranged."

She stiffened beneath his touch but did not move away. "That is noble of you, Lord Glenbrooke, but it is a totally unnecessary gesture."

"It is not noble, Lucy, my love. You know very well it is what I want. If only you can find it in your heart to forgive me this hurt I've caused you."

"You have a very persuasive tongue. No doubt you have used it to advantage on many an occasion."

He gave a little gasp of exasperation and slid his arms around her waist, holding her close. "Surely you cannot have stopped loving me. It cannot be such a shallow emotion."

She gave a little strangled laugh and disengaged his arm from about her waist. She turned to face him, her eyes ablaze with fury. "How glibly you talk of love, my lord. Surely it is greed you really mean. You are relying on my greed to remain here as the Countess of Glenbrooke, a position to which I am now accustomed, and it is your greed to have the inheritance I have been promised. You are hoping my greed will equal yours."

He stared at her increduously. "By all means be angry, Lucy. Be hurt too. Heaven knows you are entitled to feel both. But do not accuse me of that. If you will but cast your mind back, you will recall the day we visited the abbey ruin. It was nearly four weeks ago. I only learned of the new will less than a hour ago."

"You had to keep me happy and unsuspicious even then," she answered in a broken voice. She raised two hands to her head and whirled round so she could not see him. "I am confused. I only know the man I thought I loved does not really exist. The man I see before me is a plausible liar, and if you can deceive me in one way it is possible you can deceive me in another."

"I have never lied to you," he said softly, "nor have I ever pleaded with a woman as I am pleading with you now."

"Never has so much been at stake." She was near to tears and determined not to let him see it. "Please leave me, Lord Glenbrooke. I must be alone for a while so I may collect my thoughts."

He touched her arm gently but elicited no response. "I don't want to leave you alone just now."

"I have no desire for company."

"It is nearly time for luncheon. Please let me escort you downstairs."

She drew herself up straight. "Be pleased to excuse me from luncheon, my lord. I have no taste for food as you will appreciate." Adding in a more piteous voice, "Please, please leave me alone a while."

Reluctantly he said, "Very well, Lucy. But please do not be hard on me, for I do love you, and if you will but let me I swear I will spend my life making amends to you for this wrong."

She remained silent and motionless, her back ramrod straight as he backed reluctantly towards the door, and the moment it had clicked into place behind him, Lucinda's proud demeanour crumpled and she sank down on to the precious counterpane. It had lain across the royal bed for three centuries, and now she was allowing her heartbreak to pour all over it in a stream of never-ending tears.

At last her sobs abated. She sat up and wiped her damp cheeks on the hem of her gown. She wandered across to the window and stared out without really seeing anything of the beauty of the scene before her. Looking out of any of the house's windows had afforded her nothing but pleasure in the past. Now she suffered an all-consuming pain. The birds in the trees, the deer in the park, and even her own dear little lamb that frisked in the fields, belonged, but not Lucinda.

Somewhere nearby a housemaid sang happily as she worked, emphasising the misery Lucinda knew just then. A little voice told her she had no right to all the things she had taken for granted. She had no rights at Glenbrooke Abbey, yet she knew her heart would always remain here, shattered because of the earl's treachery and lying kisses.

How right, she mused, Lieutenant Stacey had been when he said the Glenbrookes were treacherous. How she wished now she had heeded his warning before it was too late to save her poor heart from its present misery.

"Lieutenant Stacey!" she cried aloud. "He will know how to help me. Has he not already said so?"

As she rushed across the room she caught sight of herself in the mirror and halted in front of it. She smoothed the skirt of her yellow muslin gown, and stared at it thoughtfully for a moment or two.

"No wonder I am wearing Melissa's clothes," she gasped. "There was no trunk of my own to lose."

As she resumed her flight across the room into the spacious dressing room, she was fumbling with the fastenings of her gown. In the cupboards of the dressing room she located the brown kerseymere gown in which she had travelled and she looked at it in disgust. Lucinda had no doubt it was her gown, for it was shabby beyond compare.

Further rummaging in the cupboards yielded up a pair of worn kid slippers, a shabby pelisse and an exceedingly ugly chip-straw hat. At the sight of them Lucinda sank back against the wall and began to cry anew.

Brushing away her tears as she did so, she put on the old clothes and, taking the cloakbag which she had discovered pushed in the corner of one cupboard, she hurried back into the main room.

When she had reached the door she paused and, with tears blurring her eyes once more, Lucinda took one glance around her. She opened the door slowly and peered up and down the corridor, and when she had made sure it was empty, she hurried out and along to the back stairs.

When she reached the outside of the house she paused to ascertain in which direction she should go to reach Lansdown Manor. Although she had passed the entrance but once during a ride out one day in Melissa's carriage, she reckoned she could find her way there again. Once she had decided in which direction she should go, she pushed away all thoughts of the happy times she had experienced during the past few weeks, and with one tear-blurred glance backwards, she hurried towards her destination.

Chapter Eleven

Despite the unusually turbulent nature of his emotions, the earl had this evening dressed with his usual care. It would have been difficult for anyone to detect his inner anxiety were it not for his ceaseless pacing up and down the drawing room floor, pausing only long enough to glance at his watch from time to time.

When the footman opened the door he paused and looked round hopefully, only to discover that it was his mother who was being ushered inside.

She hesitated as the door was closed behind her. "Am I early after all?" she asked, glancing around her. "I was sure I was exceedingly late as usual."

"A little only, Mother," he answered irritably, asking immediately, "Have you seen Lucy this evening? She is always so punctual."

The countess came across to him. "No, dearest. I dared not seek her out after you had gone to speak to her. Have you not seen her since then? I dare say she was with Uncle Percival."

The earl frowned. "No, she was not with him. He has not seen her since this morning; he told me so when I spoke to him not an hour ago as he went to his rooms."

"You *did* speak to her?"

He nodded. "I am relieved," she said, with a sigh.

"Your relief may be premature." At her alarmed look he added, "In short, Mother, she was most distressed, which was not unnatural, and she asked to be left alone. I did leave her, but it was with the utmost reluctancy."

"It was for the best," said the countess soothingly, pressing the tips of her fingers together.

"Yes," agreed her son, "I too thought she needed time alone to gather her thoughts, but now I am not so sure."

"You are going to marry her anyway, so there is nothing for her to sulk about for long."

"You are very naive, Mother. Lucy is a very sensitive person, more so than most. She is incapable of treating this light-heartedly, and I for one cannot blame her."

His mother immediately became remorseful and concerned. "Have you attempted to speak with her since?"

"No. I have had no chance. Threadlow accosted me just after I left her, and I was engaged with him for most of the afternoon discussing some accounts which were of a trifling nature. When I returned, I knocked on the door to Lucy's room. There was no reply. I assumed she still did not want to see me, but normally she is one of the first to come down to dinner. . . ."

The countess nodded, going to the door. "I cannot credit that she would sulk all this time. She has too much common-sense, but I shall go along and see her and bring her down, dearest, never you fear. It is time I tried to make amends for my part in this."

She returned no more than five minutes later although to her son her absence seemed a much longer one. He stared across the room the moment he clapped eyes on his mother's white face and wide, frightened eyes.

"Dareth, she is gone!"

"Are you sure?"

She nodded quickly and then began to speak breathlessly. "There was no reply to my knock so I took the liberty of going inside. She was nowhere to be found. Fraser hasn't seen her either. When she knocked there was no reply either and so she assumed that Lucinda had managed to dress with the help of one of the maids, which is often the case."

"Fraser had no business to assume anything."

The countess waved an impatient hand in the air. "We cannot blame Fraser. Lucinda doesn't like to wait and Fraser was late this evening.

You can't expect her to attend both of us in the same space of time as she would need for one."

"But what of Lucy?" he insisted, waving away her explanation.

"One of the housemaids thought she saw her going down the back stairs hours ago. It must have been just after you'd spoken to her. The girl didn't quite realise who it was because Lucinda has only taken the clothes she came in, but as soon as I heard, I knew it was her. What are we to do?"

He passed one hand across his face. He looked unbelievably tired. "I should have foreseen this. I should have done if I hadn't been so distressed myself."

He turned away, his mind working frantically. He gripped hard on the back of a chair as his mother said, "She cannot have gone far. She has no money. Where can she have gone?"

"Where, indeed," echoed her son. Suddenly he thumped the back of the chair with one fist and, turning sharply, he hurried across the room. "I'll wager she's gone to Stacey at Lansdown Manor."

The countess hurried after him, making a vain attempt to keep up with his long-legged stride. "Do you really believe so?" she asked as he snapped his fingers at one of the footmen, saying sharply, "My horse. As quickly as you please."

As the man hurried off to obey, another flunkey helped his lordship into his caped riding coat. "As you say, Mother, she has no money. Where else would she go? But I must hurry. Too much time has elapsed already. If Stacey learns she is an heiress he will lose no time in taking out a special licence, and she is distressed enough to follow him blindly."

He accepted his hat, gloves and riding whip from the footman. "Do be careful, Dareth," his mother begged. "And I do hope you may be in time."

The earl looked grim. "Rest assured, I will be, or Lucinda will be a widow before she has a chance to be a wife!"

The three-mile walk to Lansdown Manor seemed a very long one to Lucinda. The sun had chosen to be at its hottest today, and after becoming accustomed to the cool muslins and calicos of her borrowed wardrobe, the brown kerseymere was hot and uncomfortable. The heaviness of her heart was repeated in the heaviness of her feet in their ill-fitting shoes as she trudged disconsolately along, and all the while afraid that at any time she might be overtaken and forced to go back to Glenbrooke Abbey.

At every thought of her life there she struggled to divert her mind. How she longed to believe that the earl did really love her, and yet a little voice constantly reminded her that he was a liar, that his kisses had been only to keep her from suspecting his treachery, and his last passionate declaration a means to obtain Percival Courtney-

Smythe's money. She would rather endure a life of slavery than a marriage of that sort.

Lucinda, despite the weariness both of her body and spirit, ran the last few yards to the front door. Lansdown Manor was an imposing building constructed quite recently of red stone, although it was neither as large nor as handsome as Glenbrooke Abbey.

Now she was at her destination new doubts assailed her. Perhaps Lieutenant Stacey, when he learned of her situation in life, would not want to see her, but, as she raised her hand to the bell pull, she knew she had no choice. There was no one else to whom she could turn. Everyone at Glenbrooke Abbey would conspire to keep her there.

A frosty-looking butler eyed her disapprovingly when she stated her business. Nevertheless he asked with a practised politeness, "Whom shall I say is calling, madam?"

Lucinda swallowed hard. "Tell him it is . . . Lady Glenbrooke."

The butler's eyes widened slightly and his demeanour softened perceptibly but Lucinda fancied she detected a grin on the face of one of the footmen.

"If you will but come this way, my lady," said the butler, "I will inform Lieutenant Stacey you are here."

Lucinda was ushered into a small reception room where she waited impatiently, unable to keep herself from pacing up and down the floor, and it was only a few minutes later that the lieutenant came hurrying in.

"Lady Glenbrooke!" he cried, looking at her in some astonishment. "What brings you here in such a way? You are alone I perceive."

"Yes, entirely alone," she managed to say. She went up to him. He took her trembling hands in his and she said, "I am in such a fix, Lieutenant Stacey. I did not know anyone else to whom I could turn for help."

Looking intrigued, as well he might be, he led her to a sofa where they both sat down. He raised both her hands to his lips and said, "I am deeply moved at the honour you have afforded me, Lady Glenbrooke, but delighted as I am, this visit is extremely ill-considered. Glenbrooke may misconstrue your motives."

"Oh, please do not call me Lady Glenbrooke! I am not Lady Glenbrooke. I am Lucinda Kendricks. I am not his wife, so he cannot misconstrue anything I do!"

Lieutenant Stacey drew back sharply, his eyes narrowing. "What is this?"

Lucinda withdrew her hands, very concious of her real status, and began to explain, haltingly, pausing frequently to swallow her tears, whilst the lieutenant's expression turned from surprise to incredulity and then to anger.

"So you see," she ended, "it was all to hoax Great Uncle Percival—oh, heavens, he is not that to me!—and Mr Courtney-Smythe has made me his heiress."

"It is no more than justice that he has done so." He then drew himself up straight. "That scoundrel. The villain! How dare he use you so, Miss Kendricks! How dare he shame one so fair to achieve his own wicked ends. As if any amount of fortune could justify misusing you."

He rose indignantly to his feet. "I shall avenge your honour forthwith, Miss Kendricks. Have no fear on that score; I shall draw blood."

Her eyes opened wide in alarm. "Oh no! Please do not even think of calling him out, I beseech you. I cannot allow this matter to end in bloodshed. Besides," she added, remembering the occasion he had instructed her, to the countess's outrage, to handle a pistol, "I have seen Glenbrooke at pistol practice. He is a crack shot, Lieutenant Stacey; and a cooler head I've never seen."

He needed no further dissuasion and, sinking down on to the settee again, took her hands once more and held them close to his breast. "It shall be as you wish, my dear Miss Kendricks. For myself I would call him out in a trice, but now I perceive worry on my account would only burden you further. And you do need a protector now. I am only thankful you were wise enough to come to me. I fear for your safety."

"Oh no, Lieutenant Stacey. Glenbrooke would not harm me."

"You are charitable indeed," he answered

grimly. "For myself I am convinced he is a villain indeed, and you stand between him and a fortune." He smiled with grim satisfaction. "I'll wager Mr Courtney-Smythe did not consider that aspect." Lucinda was staring at him wide-eyed, and then she turned away. "Did I not say I feared some mischief? But I confess I did not believe even Glenbrooke capable of such infamy as this."

"You were wiser than I," she murmured in a broken voice.

"I always considered it odd that he never addressed you as Lady Glenbrooke or as 'my wife.' He always called you 'Lucy,'" he laughed and she could have cried at hearing the earl's own name for her, "just like any middle-class merchant."

She raised her eyes then. "Will you be kind enough to lend me enough money to enable me to return to London, Lieutenant Stacey? I shall ensure it is repaid to you however long it takes me to do so."

He looked bemused. "London, Miss Kendricks? You wish to go to London?"

"I wish to return to the orphan asylum. I dare say the Mrs Purvey who had engaged me to serve her has now engaged some other person in my stead."

He gave a harsh laugh. "You shall serve no one, Miss Kendricks! Have you forgotten that you are heiress to a very large fortune?"

She shook her head. "No, I have not forgotten but it is not my entitlement. I do not want it."

The lieutenant looked profoundly shocked. "It is indeed your entitlement, Miss Kendricks. Mr Courtney-Smythe has expressly said so. In his lowest hour he wanted you to be his heiress. It is possible that the illness was induced just to force him to make a will in Glenbrooke's favour. Mr Courtney-Smythe has good sense ideed, more so if he leaves Glenbrooke Abbey as soon as he can. Although they are hardly likely to poison him now. You would be the only one to benefit by *that*."

Lucinda looked at him in horror. "Surely the earl and countess cannot be so wicked as to do that."

"The illness was decidedly opportune. But," he went on fervently, "you need have no fear. You are safe now and I am pledged to protect you with my own life."

She said nothing, her mind was full of this new horror and before she had any chance to recover from it he went on, his voice filled with urgency, "Miss Kendricks, I saw you at Glenbrooke Abbey and was entranced by you, you must know that." He ignored her reddening cheeks. "This situation, however distressing to you, is the answer to my wicked prayer. Each time I clapped eyes on you I could only wish you were not married to a man who quite obviously had no regard for you. . . ."

"Was it so obvious?" she asked.

"Was it not obvious to you, Miss Kendricks?" She lowered her eyes in acknowledgement, and he held her hands more tightly. "Miss Kendricks, I have worshipped you from the moment I first set eyes on you. I beg of you allow me the honour of making you my wife. No one shall ever know of this shame Glenbrooke has heaped upon one so fair."

"Lieutenant Stacey!"

"Allow me to convey you to my home this day, where we can obtain a special licence and be married almost immediately. The fact that you have been compromised most unfairly means nothing to me."

"But what of your brother and Melissa? They believe me Glenbrooke's wife."

"They both have a care for their good name. Any mention of Glenbrooke's infamy will tarnish that, so nothing will be said, and Melissa will love you. Indeed, she already does. She will welcome you most cordially. Certainly, Glenbrooke will be glad to forget the incident, even if he cannot forget he failed miserably in what he attempted to do."

Lucinda sighed, and he said, "You fulfilled the role of a countess most admirably, Miss Kendricks. You were meant to live the life of a lady." His voice grew lower and more urgent, "You cannot wish to return to your former way of life."

"I cannot even remember it," she sighed.

He stood up, letting her hands go. "Give me but

a few minutes to make my apologies to my host, and to have my carriage brought round and we shall leave here with no more delay. For your sake I am anxious to avoid a confrontation with Glenbrooke."

Lucinda watched him hurry from the room. She had come hoping only for help in reaching London, not dreaming that his feelings for her were so profound. She sank back into the sofa. Of course, it was true she had no fancy to return to a life she couldn't even remember, and in agreeing to marry Lieutenant Stacey, for whom she had the highest regard, she would at least be making an admirable man happy....

The earl also considered the journey to Lansdown Manor an unending one. He jumped from his horse almost before the animal had stopped. Impatiently he pulled at the bell twice before the butler, as unhurried as ever, appeared to answer it.

"Is Lieutenant Stacey at home?" he asked, almost before he was in the hall.

"No, my lord. Lieutenant Stacey left some hours ago."

The earl muttered an oath beneath his breath and, slapping his whip against the palm of his gloved hand, asked sharply, "Was he alone?"

"No, my lord. He was with . . . er . . . Lady Glenbrooke." When the earl made no reply and instead stared fiercely into the corner of the hall, the butler ventured, "Shall I fetch my master, my lord?"

The earl roused himself and became more urbane. "By no means disturb him while he is at his dinner." He considered the servant for a moment or two before removing a coin from his purse. "What is your name, my man?"

"Datchett, my lord."

"Well, Datchett," he said, tossing the coin idly into the air, "is it possible for you to obtain one or two items for me?"

The butler looked unperturbed. "If it is at all possible, my lord. What are these items, if I may be so bold as to ask?"

The earl explained quickly and without so much as raising an eyebrow a fraction, the butler said, "I believe I know just where I may lay my hand on such items as you describe, my lord."

The earl tossed the coin again. "There'll be two of these for you if you are back within five minutes."

"I shall be back in less than four, my lord."

It was already growing dark. Lucinda sat bolt upright next to Lieutenant Stacey inside his extremely well-sprung and luxuriously fitted coach. No words had passed between them since their stop for dinner at an inn along the road a short time before. Lucinda was only aware that with every mile they travelled, she was going further and further away from Dareth, and when she saw him again it would be as the wife of Lieutenant Stacey.

He glanced at her and smiled fondly. "You ate very little, my dear. Are you not hungry?"

"I have no appetite," she answered in a dull voice, wondering how in the circumstances he could have partaken of such a hearty meal. "I imagine I am unused to such lavishly furnished tables at the orphan asylum."

He patted her hand sympathetically. "Put that all behind you, my love. It would be as well for you not to mention it again. From now onwards you will enjoy the very best of everything. As soon as we are married we shall leave for London where the foremost dressmakers shall be yours to command."

She was about to say something but he was lost in his own thoughts. "And then you shall set Brighton ablaze with your loveliness. We shall take a house there and entertain everyone of consequence, including the Prince of Wales with whom I can claim acquaintance. Our routs will be talked about for years to come, I guarantee. You shall be Society's foremost hostess. Glenbrooke will see the splendid results of his scheming. We have a good deal to thank him for."

Lucinda looked anxious. "I was terribly distraught this afternoon. Now I have had a chance to consider it, it may be possible he tried to make amends. Perhaps I judged him too harshly."

The lieutenant laughed. "Being aware of your

gentle and trusting nature, Miss Kendricks, it is very likely not."

At the sound of a noise very much like a pistol shot, both passengers became alert. The horses began to slow and the lieutenant looked around him helplessly.

"Damnation! In the rush to leave the Manor I forgot my pistols."

"Surely we are not unarmed?" asked Lucinda in alarm.

"The driver is armed but he is not so good a shot as I."

As he spoke there came another shot. "But we have nothing worth stealing."

Lieutenant Stacey moved to open the door. "Let us hope we can persuade this fellow of the fact."

But, as he opened the door to the carriage, he found that a pair of pistols were pointing at his chest. Lucinda remained in the carriage, pressing herself into the leather upholstery, hoping she would not be noticed.

"Both of you out on to the road," ordered the highwayman who, in the dusk, was a sinister figure enveloped in a muffler, battered beaver hat and a grease-stained frieze coat. Lucinda edged forward slowly as Lieutenant Stacey held out his hand to her.

"Where's yer pistols?" demanded a rough voice.

"I have none," answered the lieutenant. "We are carrying no valuables either," he added as he handed Lucinda down. The driver and postilions were standing, hands raised against the side of the coach, and the driver's pistol, she noticed, was lying in the bushes.

"Yer carriage proclaims yer a man of means. . . ."

"We left hurriedly and had no time to bring anything of value."

"And the lady?"

The highwayman glanced at Lucinda, who shivered a little. The evening had grown cool. She wished she had not been so impetuous in leaving Glenbrooke Abbey. She felt sure that if the earl were here, he would make short work of this rogue.

"She has none," answered the lieutenant, his voice betraying his own fear.

The highwayman raised the pistols a little higher and Lucinda gave out a little cry of alarm. "I'll fill yer full o' lead if yer lyin' to me."

The lieutenant began to move backwards until he bumped into Lucinda. "You may have the guineas from my purse and my watch and fobs, but there is nothing else, I assure you."

The rogue kept the pistols levelled at Lieutenant Stacey and looked again at Lucinda. "I fancy that the lady will be carrying a fortune in jewels somewhere about her person."

The lieutenant gave a little sigh of exasperation. "Does she look as if she might? Take what little I possess and let us on our way."

The highwayman continued to gaze at Lucinda

who was looking at the ground. "A gentry cove's woman always has rubies and diamonds, unless, of course," he added maliciously to the lieutenant, "the dandies have taken to travellin' with abigails."

The lieutenant drew himself up, pulling indignantly at his waistcoat as Lucinda could not help but giggle, which she strove hard to hide. The highwayman put one of his pistols away, much to her relief, but the relief was short lived. He held out his free hand to her.

"Shake yer shambles, ma'am. Climb up along with me."

She looked up sharply and the lieutenant started forward, but was arrested by the pistol being levelled in the direction of his waistcoat.

"You'll get lead in yer breadbasket if yer come a mite closer."

Lucinda looked to him for help but received none. She shook her head frenziedly. "I beg you, sir, believe me, I have no jewellery or anything else of value."

She put out one hand which to her surprise he gripped and as she screamed in alarm he pulled her up in front of him with no effort at all.

"You'll fetch a heap of ransom, I'll be bound," he said in her ear. "You've a look of a runaway pair about yer and someone'll pay for you, m'beauty."

She turned and tried to slap his face but even with one hand he managed to hold her helpless.

"You'll regret this," warned a red-faced Lieutenant Stacey.

As the highwayman urged his horse forward, he answered with a laugh, "I'll not regret the ten thousand guineas you'll pay to get her back."

"*Ten* thousand guineas!" exclaimed the lieutenant. "I cannot find such an amount, you rogue."

The highwayman laughed again. "Then I'll find someone who will, or I'll keep her myself."

So saying, the highwayman rode off with his prize. The lieutenant lost as little time as his injured leg would allow in diving for the pistol the driver had dropped. He levelled it at the highwayman and fired, but missed; the highwayman was already enveloped in the fast encroaching dusk.

The lieutenant stared after them, scratching at his head in vexation. "That horse," he murmured a moment later, "it was a fine bit of blood for a highwayman to ride, and I'll be dashed if I haven't seen it before somewhere. . . ."

Lucinda fought her way out of folds of unconciousness to hear a very familiar voice say, in an extremely worried way, "Thank heavens, all is well. She is recovering from her swoon at last."

She struggled to sit up, pushing aside the hand that held a vinaigrette beneath her nose. For a few seconds she peered around her in a bemused way, and then she looked to the countess who was bending over her anxiously, with the earl sitting at the end of the sofa.

"How did I come to be here?" she asked, still in considerable confusion.

"You must relax," answered the earl, who was looking extremely discomforted.

"I cannot relax! How did you wrest me from that rogue?"

The countess hurried across the room. "I think I shall ask Cook to make some broth, my dear. You must be famished. I'll wager not a morsel has passed your lips since breakfast."

"Oh please do not trouble," she cried, desperate not to be left alone with the earl, but the countess had already gone.

The moment they were alone he moved further up the sofa to sit at her side. "Lie still awhile. You fainted away completely."

"I was excessively afraid of that vile creature. He threatened to keep me for himself. I suppose I should be glad that he did not do so. Money has a greater attraction. Did he ransom me to you? Lieutenant Stacey did not have ten thousand guineas."

At this the earl threw back his head and laughed, and she added in hurt tones, "No doubt I was an investment to you, but I wish you might have left me with him. He was less of a rogue than you."

"Do you really believe so?" He laughed, again.

"You'll get lead in yer breadbasket if yer come a mite closer," he said roughly.

She gasped and sat up sharply. "It was *you!* Oh, you wicked, wicked man. You frightened me half to death."

"I did not mean to," he said, the amusement going from his eyes, "although I did hope to put some fear into Stacey. But I did not expect to cause you to swoon and I beg your forgiveness."

"But why did you do it?"

"If I hadn't disguised myself you would have refused to come with me."

"Certainly I would."

"And I had no time to argue uselessly. I had already missed my dinner."

Lucinda's lips tightened into a thin line. "You are even more villainous than I believed."

He took her hand and kissed it. "No, my love, just desperately in love." She continued to stare at him, too stunned to withdraw her hand. "If you tell me you truly care for Lieutenant Stacey I shall return you to him immediately, but admit it, Lucy, you would far rather be with me than him."

She sank back into the cushions, still keeping her hand in his. "Oh, yes I would. If I am to be married for Mr Courtney-Smythe's wedding gift I had far rather it be you. He had it half spent before we had reached Hinckley."

The earl laughed again. "How typical that is. I suspected his motive was not a humanitarian one. But you should know by now that I do not want

Great Uncle Percival's wedding gift. You are all I care for. You may do with it what you wish."

She brightened. "Oh, do you really mean it?"

"We shall contrive very well without it, Lucy. Both you and I have discovered together a liking for the simple, country life."

She sank back into the cushions once again. "I could buy a great many comforts for the children of the orphan asylum with that money. They have so few."

"That is an excellent idea, Lucy. You can become a patroness."

He stopped speaking abruptly and stared at her. In fact they stared at each other for a good few moments and then she said in wonderment, "I remember everything, Dareth. It's as if I had never forgotten."

"Thank goodness," he said, sighing profoundly. "All must be clear between us from now on."

"I fell asleep on the top of the stage and must have fallen off when it stopped suddenly. I feel a curtain in my mind has been lifted at last and I can see behind it. I was so incomplete before. There was so much I didn't understand about myself."

"Do you still regard me as a villain?"

She smiled and shook her head. "Your action in bringing me here was a kindly one, and you have tried to make amends for the countess's mistake. Even when you gave me such a fright this evening it resulted in my memory coming back."

"Now I can arrange a wedding as soon as it can be contrived."

Her smile faded. "No, Dareth, you mustn't do that. I couldn't allow you to do it. It wouldn't be right."

He made a gesture of impatience. "Surely you still cannot believe my intent is mercenary."

Her eyes opened wide. "Oh no. I realise you have become very fond of me and I am grateful for it. I was a fool to run away tonight. It was only hurt pride that caused me to do so, not a fear that you wanted me for my money."

"Then why would our marriage not be right? I have already taken the liberty of asking my great uncle to remain for the ceremony."

Lucinda gave a broken little laugh. "Have you forgotten my upbringing? I am not worthy of you."

"I have not forgotten. I simply regard it as unimportant, and if you recall so does everyone else who has accepted you already. No, Lucy, you do not escape me so easily."

She smiled at him. "I do not wish to, although I feel I am reckless in admitting it."

"We Farringdons are reckless, every last one of us."

"Will Lieutenant Stacey truly remain silent on this matter?"

The earl looked momentarily grim. "I am sure he will. By the time we see him again we will be married. No one will believe such a tall story if he chooses to repeat it. After all, his action tonight did not quite enhance his reputation as a hero. He was trembling in his boots. He will remain silent."

Lucinda stifled a laugh with her one free hand. "He said the same of you. Everyone will have such red faces if this matter is made public, so no one will speak of it. How splendid it is!"

"Did you see his face when you asked him if he had an abigail?"

"No. As a matter of fact, I was watching yours. Just now, I am doing the same to see if you are recovered."

"Oh, yes I am."

"Good, because I am going to kiss you before we are interrupted. However much I protest, I have the feeling you are going to be heavily chaperoned from this day until the day we are married."

Lucinda did not demur and a few minutes later when she was able, she said contentedly, laying her head against his shoulder, "How fortunate I am that Mrs Purvey did not deem me worthy of a seat inside the coach, Dareth. . . ."